James Robertson

Orellana and other poems

James Robertson

Orellana and other poems

ISBN/EAN: 9783337207113

Printed in Europe, USA, Canada, Australia, Japan

Cover: Foto ©Andreas Hilbeck / pixelio.de

More available books at **www.hansebooks.com**

ORELLANA

AND

OTHER POEMS

ORELLANA

AND

OTHER POEMS

BY

J. LOGIE ROBERTSON, M.A.

WILLIAM BLACKWOOD AND SONS
EDINBURGH AND LONDON
MDCCCLXXXI

APOLOGY FOR POESY.

From what far regions of the Infinite
   Beyond the solar glow
I have been sent from uncreated light,
And why to this dim borderland of Night,
   My Lord, I do not know.

But Thou art wise; and in my mortal sphere,
   Pent in this prison tower,
Blown to me from my spirit-home I hear,
Sounding, now faint and far, now near and
     clear,
   Harmonies every hour.

The sun goes surging up the East in song :
   The moon in muffled strain
Repeats the pæan, whispering it among
The choral stars, that listen and prolong,
   And cease and sing again.

Ocean all through his many-chambered seas,
  The seas through all their bays,
Rivers and rills, forests with all their trees,
Tempest, and thunder, and the wandering breeze,
  My God, proclaim Thy praise.

—And oft when midnight buries vale and hill,
  Loosening its music free,
My heart instinctive sings, as sea-shells will,
Though inland carried far, faithfully still
  Echo their parent sea.

These are of Thee—these broken harmonies,
  That wander from Thy lyre
Like wind-blown blossoms of the Hesperides,
Or spray sun-kissed to golden irises
  And twists of coloured fire.

I hear and thrill;—not as the soulless cliff
  Deaf to the vocal sea,
But answering to the joy like dancing skiff:
—God of all Harmony! forgive me if
  I dare to answer Thee!

CONTENTS.

ORELLANA.

BRIERS.

FROM THE SICILIAN OF VICORTAI.

SYLVÆ.

CONTENTS.

SONNETS.

NORWEGIAN SONNETS.

ORELLANA

A POEM

BOOK I.

PERU was fallen, and her king was dead;
And from its tower, plucked down with ruth-
    less hand,
The golden image of the worshipped Sun
No longer blazed o'er Cuzco. Far and wide
The land was harried of its garnered wealth,
Stripped of its ornaments of dowried gold,
Its silver from the rock's reluctant grip
Wrung with relentless hand; and what re-
    mained
Was the slow promise of the laboured fields.
But not to them, these fiery youth of Spain,
The shepherd's even pulse, or the long hopes
That wait on tillage and the swelling seed

And fostering heat and rain : their veins were
    filled
With lust of conquest, and the gleam of gold
Was ever in each eye. Yet still they thronged
The narrow belt between the aerial hills
And the wide mystery of the Western seas ;
And, finding nothing left of native growth
To fuel their ambitious wants, they turned
With envious glances on each other's gain.
Till the great Marquis, sitting at Quito,
And ruling with an ill-acknowledged sway
Subjects that hoped each one himself to rule,
Spoke to Gonzalo :

            " Other realms there are
Beyond these giant hills or o'er those waves,
Haply in continent, at least in isle,
The bearer of whose destiny be thou
And these—take whom thou wilt—that cannot
    rest
Until it be delivered. Oh, my brother !
There comes not once again in after-time
To thee or any man such glorious hope

As beckons now : 'tis the last mystery
Of the round globe hid in yon ocean waste,
Or from yon snowy heights to be descried.
Rise equal to thy fortune.   Be it thine
To finish what Columbus but began,
And   make   the   name,   our   common   name,
  Pizarro,
Wide as the water, lasting as the land !
See what a sacrifice of fame I make !
But thou or I, what matter?   We are one ;
And while I strengthen yet my foothold here
The freer thine for conquest."
      While he spake,
Down the steep flanks of the Sierra crept
The tell-tale breezes, bearing in their wings
Odours of cinnamon, and whispering low
Of wealth unguarded in the vales beyond.
The Spanish soldier, keeping nightly watch
Before the general's tent with idle pace,
Paused, and with upturned face inquiringly
Sniffed the cool odorous air : sweeter to him
Its soft caresses on his swarthy cheek

Than memories of Xenil, or the gush
Of Ebro's waters clear : nor kindlier less
Its freshness folding round his sunburnt neck
Than virgin's arm of snow.   While thus he
    stood,
Gonzalo, issuing from the tent, remarked
His absent gaze upon the snowy ridge
Which cut into the sky, shearing the stars,
Past the low-floating moon.   Familiarly
Upon his shoulder with broad hand he smote,
And to his look high thought attributing—
"What say'st thou, comrade?   Will it yield to
    Spain ?
Or is it sacred to the stars alone,
A higher Alp than Hannibal would dare?
Perchance there is a Hannibal at hand !
Only be ready thou, my valiant soldier,
Whom I elect my standard-bearer here
—What is thy name?"
                 Abrupt he stayed ; and he,
That other,—" Hernan Sanchez am I called."
" I know thee well : attend my trumpet-call

To-morrow morning; I have need of thee "—
And passed to his own tent, leaving the youth
With the warm blush of pride upon his face,
And a vague sense of praise.

                    At earliest dawn
Gonzalo's trumpet shrilling through the tents
Awoke the warrior conquering in his dreams.
Three hundred youths sprang joyful to the
    call.
These overnight, ere e'er he had retired,
And with his great idea burning clear
In its unclouded dawn, Gonzalo drew,
As flame draws flame, partakers of a faith
To light on hidden empire, win for Spain
Another Mexico, a new Peru !
Each brought a heart strengthened by hardy
    use,
And never yet contaminate with fear ;
A sword, and each could wield it ; and a band
Of dusky faces waiting on his nod,
And catching from his frown the fearlessness
Born of excessive or habitual fear.

With arms caught up in haste, and warlike
    stores,

And other needs resigned to Indian slaves

Enlackeyed with the baggage, forth at dawn,

With little words of parting,—forth they rode

While yet the ensanguined sun, like some vast
    bird

With flaming wings in a wide equipoise,

Stooped on the mountains ere he soared aloft

For a strong flight prepared : not otherwise

The soul of each, with vigorous thoughts elate,

Spurning the summits of attainèd hope,

Looked to a loftier goal.

               Next day at noon

Their ranks were startled with a voice behind

As of a messenger who gallops hard,

Ere yet too late, with some neglected trust.

All turned ; and lo ! impelled by destiny,

Breathless he comes, the inimitable thief

Who stole the glory of the Amazon,

And wrote across a continent his name

As if on parchment with a running pen,—

Who, like a meteor flashing down the night,
That bursts full-blazed, and, blazing, is blown
 out,
That upsprings unannounced of tremulous
 dawn,
And sinks without a setting,—shot athwart
The width of the New World, and disappeared
Leaving the long lapse of the ocean stream
To syllable his name to all its shores
With repetitive murmur, Orellana !
      On the fifth day
The sudden swoop of night descending prone
Surprised them in a hollow where the land
Sinks ere it reascends with daring slope
To end with snowy purity in Heaven.
Here, weary with their march of days, the task,
Though self-imposed, in all its magnitude
First seemed to tower with sudden increment
Beyond the flight of Hope.   For, as they lay
Supine beside their camp-fires, and the moon,
Looking sheer down upon them from the ridge
With unexpected light, revealed the steeps

Which rose to where she seemed to sit en-
  throned,
And the vast bulk as of a natural wall
Which God with His own hands had built, the
  thought
Of their own littleness, as there they lay,
A handful hid in a forgotten valley,
While the great mountain towered and the
  broad sky
Spread placid and serene, and the vague fear
Of a presumptuous sin in such high presence
O'ercame them, wearied, and they would have
  fled,
But that they were ashamed even to speak
The coward thoughts which each man deemed
  his own.
But with the morn courage returned ; and Hope
That, revelling in the Elysian fields beyond,
Forgetful of her office by the way,
Had winged by night her backward flight un-
  seen,
Now settling on the summits overhead,

Shone with severer ray, commandingly

To the stern joys of danger ill to dare

And labour yielding slow.   Under its light

·(For hope too distant but fatigues the mind)

They braced them for the first encountered
     toil,

And were in wonder, past the point of shame,

Whence the distrust and awe of yesternight,—

Distrust of mind, the strongest power on earth,

And awe of senseless matter, dull and dead,

And would have laughed aloud in the clear air

Of early morning as they scaled the side

Of the huge innocent mountain, but the dread

Of a recurrence of the perilous spell

Moved them to sober thought and kept them
     mute.

   Three days the ascent continued—three long
     days—

And on the fourth they came upon the snow;

And still the mountain towered till lost to view

In a dense whirl of cloud.   Ah ! then for thee,

Poor Indian slave, struggling beneath thy load,

With back low bent and shivering limbs thin
    clad,
On the bleak wintry heights, what woes in store
When wild and wide, with whirling wind and
    snow,
And crash of loosened rocks the storm came
    down,
And, clutching at thy heart with fingers cold,
Blew the sharp ice of death into thine eyes,
That never more should brighten at the glow
Of summer beauty in thy native plains !
Unseen the mute imploring look, unrecked
If seen, with which the sinking Indian turned
His human eyes, dim with the glaze of death,
Upon his resolute lord, the Spaniard drew
His mantle closer round him, set his teeth,
And without word toiled steadily up the steep,
Nor turned to right or left, nor paused, nor
    spoke
Even when his comrade, swaying to the blast,
Went headlong o'er the rocks, or disappeared
Where, walking fearless to his doom, he stepped

Upon a bridge of snow. For he would storm

The stronghold of the storm, and plant his foot

And flag victorious in the chiefest seat

And citadel of the tempest !

                        Yet at last

When they had reached the summit the wind

    dropped,

And the mist reeled and fled : the sun poured

    in,

And shivering on the naked top, they saw

Through the immaculate air the curving globe

Bend to the far horizon's utmost verge

From west to east unknown, a roomy width !

But not beyond the grasp of human will

To limit and explore : the mystery,

The impenetrable mystery was gone

Of magnitude : the big earth seemed to shrink

To conquerable compass ; and the fear

That there was nothing further now to find,

Nor continent to conquer after this,

High-hovering o'er their minds, would have

    descended

To circumscribe their hope, but that the view
That eastward stretched beneath them filled
    their eyes,
And shut out from their hearts the after-pain,
Which yet, with furious mind swift to ex-
    haust
Immediate expectation, some even then
In lust of conquest were anticipating !
    It was a scene of Earth the grandest : far
As eye could pierce undimmed with utmost
    strain
The landscape spread in virgin loveliness
As if new-made, without the trace of man,
And waiting in the hush of afternoon
Expectant of possessors, a new race
Of sinless being, to admire its beauty
And live the life of happy worshippers
Amid its groves, and gratefully content.
    Far other they that with fierce eyes looked
    down
From the high natural wall that guarded in
This later paradise : the wolvish joy

That snatches to destroy lay in their heart
Slumbering, while wonder gazed on tiptoe mute
Where wide savannahs rolled like a green sea
Of verdure decked with flowers, and forests
    waved
Their wealth of branches on the lower hills,
And in the lonely valleys brightly clear
Wound with a noble freedom lordly streams,
With here a wide expanse of silvery lake
Green-islanded with palm of stately droop,
And there the sheeny bend repeated oft
Of some more distant river sliding slow
To far-off waters.   They forgat their toils,
Forgat that they had ever lived till now.
The past broke from them wholly, like a mantle
It slipped from them with all its care and
    grief,
Remembrance of inhospitable shores,
Hardship on hill and billow, sickness, want,
Thirst, the broad ocean, memories of home,
Country, and kin, and love's and friendship's
    claims.

They seemed new-wakened; and, the present
    pain
Of pinching cold unfelt, their souls leapt down
To taste existence in the under valleys.
  On the sharp rocks meanwhile the Indians
    lay
Breathless with pallid lips moaning in pain
Their secret miseries to Mother Earth
That would not take them to the long embrace
Of her pain-lulling arms, but let them cling
Heedless of their complaints, the while she
    flung
Her favours at the feet of aliens.
Or if, though few, in shivering groups upheld
By force of sympathy, not native might,
Incuriously like timid sheep they turned
Their dumb pathetic eyes from the new scenes
That met their adverse gaze, arrived the top,
Backwards to whence they came : it was their
    home,
And this perchance the latest farewell look
Of happiness and hope !

Night caught them thus;
These on the new-found land gazing with hope,
And those with mind or eye despondingly
Upon the old. And now along the ridge
Glimmered the little camp-fires, scantily fed
With sapless twigs in handfuls, wintry moss,
And baggage-boxes, what they best could spare.
To sleep was death : the Spaniard in his cloak
Stalked out the weary hours from fire to fire
Under the chilling shadow of the dark,
Shadow of death to many ! where they sat
Frozen to statues, stretching pulseless arms
To flames that but revealed the stony glare
Of eyes untenanted, and gave no heat ;
Or ghastlier still when the cold beam of morn
Played on the features of the seated dead
Circling a heap of ashes !

Down the long slope
At break of day the straggling march began,
And ere the last, an Indian with his load,
Had left the night's encampment to the dead,
The hovering condor dropped upon its prey.

B

Snow fell in mantling flakes, but soon they
    dipped
Into a warmer air : the grass grew green,
And plants, just budding in the sheltered cleft,
And clumps of trees in social brotherhood,
And note of startled bird, and flash of plumes
Awoke unwonted pleasure in their minds
To see and hear at hand : in one day's march
They stepped from January into June.
And still 'twas January, the drear time
When universal death to other lands
Makes periodic visit to assert
Usurped dominion o'er the realms of life
Designed of old for governance of man,
An ill-kept birthright : but in this fair land,
A new-made world then first surveyed by eyes
Tired with the faded glories of the old,
Perpetual Spring and Summer hand in hand,
Inseparable sisters, make their home
Eternal in the valleys : wintry storms
Menace but come not, nor the bounteous year
Ends in a harvestry of withered leaves,

But leaf to leaf without a pause succeeds

Shooting off death, and bud to blossom grows,

And on the bough, whence falls the fruit mature,

Straight peering through the tender bark you
    see

The hastening buds gemming the immortal tree.
  Arrived the lower slopes they pitched their
    camp

Under a lofty shade of forest boughs,

And wasted a long afternoon in doubt

Which way to turn, so wide the region lay,

In its immensity fit to maintain

The growth of ancient monarchies that might

In solitude be sitting far apart

And coexist, perchance in mutual peace

As being each to other quite unknown.

Ere early nightfall—for the western hills,

A high horizon, met the sinking sun

Before its full decline—their scouts returned

And made report of natural gardens fair,

And bird and beast that followed wildly tame

But fled them when approached, as half in fear

And half in wonder of the human form,

But nowhere trace of man or other race

Corporeal that betokened by their look

Or handiwork the godlike power of mind.

The gibbering of the ape rang through the
woods

And from the rocks and o'er the rushing
streams;

And on the lonely level river-shores

Where cities should have sat, or temple towered

On flowery hill, primeval quiet reigned :

The land was tenantless.

So on they rode with listless bridles ringing

Idly, and silence fell upon their march.

Through the clear air from boughs o'erarching
high

In sunny radiance fragile blossoms fair,

The peaceful tribute of the unowned woods,

Descended lightly on their warlike arms,

As down the glade or by the forest's marge

In a strange pomp the short procession wound.

They moved as in a dream : the industrious bee

Hummed heedless by on its own task intent

As if they were not ; on the distant glade

The indifferent herd was feeding as they
    passed ;

The bird pursued its mate from tree to tree,

Forgetful of their presence ; they were shunned

Or tolerated only in a land

Sacred to peaceful thoughts and beauteous
    forms :

The genius of the place viewed them askance,

Withholding all communion : they were awed

By the lone wealth and beauty of the land,

And felt like men of too presumptuous mind

Trespassing on the gardens of a god.

They longed for difficulties, dangers, foes,

Which yet they dreaded being yet unseen,

Yet everywhere suspected : and as oft

As to some flowery eminence they came

That rose unforested, a specular mount,

Commanding all the varied region round.

It was the sudden movement in the brake

Of panther half-revealed, or to the shore

The alligator shooting from the stream,

That sent the languor from their sated eyes,

O'erwearied with the spectral loveliness

And dulled by the excess of beauty,—if perchance

The distant figure might betoken man,

Savage or civilised, urging the chase

Afoot, or in canoe threading the maze

Of intertangling waters that unite

Haply some hidden settlement or hut

With the big bustle of a central town.

Strange choice of men, if choice it may be
called,

Perverse that inappreciative turns

Or with suspicious eye from the green nooks

Of Eden that still gem the desolate earth

To fix on barren sands and snowy wastes

And rocks amid the sea : strange choice is
theirs

Self-exiled in the wild to force by art,

And hardly force after long strife and pain,

A pittance from inhospitable shores

Among unlovely scenes, while nature wastes

Her richest and her fairest on the brute.

As lovely is the land, and still, alas !

As lonely to this day, as when they passed,

These mailèd strangers, like a threatening wing

That hurries through the sunshine of a dream.

Yet still the Briton to his barren rocks

Clings with convulsive hand !   It seems as if,

Since the great nameless terror of the Flame

That round the umbrageous gates of Eden
    swung

Relentless to the expatriated pair,

The memory of the fear, an instinct grown

Transmitted with the blood, still drives the sons

Of Adam to the Desert, and despoils

With strange suspicions loveliness itself

Of more than half its natural yield of joy.

So through those beauteous realms, that seemed
    to them

The hallowed gardens of an absent god,

With fearful hearts they hastened.   And ere long

Strange fitful airs of most divine perfume,

That come and go like wandered harmonies
Loosed from an angel's lyre, salute their sense
Inhaling Paradise ;—the heralds these
Of a new marvel from the hidden East.
And lo ! at last she comes, the fair Wind-
    queen,
Riding the billowy air most gracefully !
The tall tree-tops in meek obeisance bow,
The lower forest claps its hands of leaves,
And the dim air is lightened with the flush
And glow of scattered blossoms, pink and pale,
Before her coming ! She is come, is gone !
And the sweet thought of cedarn palaces
And bowers of cinnamon in far retreats
Amid the woodland gloom fills all the mind,
Dropped from her trailing garments as she
    passed,
Till growing faint and faint the charm dies out,
And to the hungering Spaniard leaves again
The common airs of earth, and memories
Eternal, though of momentary birth.
    Now with the heavenly balm intoxicate

They turn their quest to whence the incense
    came,
If haply they may find the odorous shades
Of El Dorado : sudden hope is theirs
Expectant of fruition every hour,
But every hour the hope is lengthened out,
And fond exertion slackens; droopingly
They journey on as in a labyrinth
Whose every winding leads them towards an
    end,
Or leaves them more astray : forward they
    move,
Yet more like wearied soldiers to their camp
Listless returning after a defeat.
    The vacant air transmits no messages,
Or, from perplexing quarters faintly blown,
The musky-pinioned couriers of the sky,
Viewless and vagrant, only mock their toil ;
For everywhere the land is as before,
Beauteous but barren of immediate gain ;
And the long calm eventless monotone
Of day succeeds to day with all the hues

That at the first flashed in their joyous eyes
Now faded, blanched, and colourless as glass
On which the shivered lance of level light,
Full aimed, no longer falls.

              " A soldier I,"
At length impatiently the leader spoke :
'Twas midnight, and the restless Spaniards sat
Like statues, speaking none, beneath the shade
Of the mysterious wood, while overhead
Pulsed the large constellations in the heat
Of the high air most tranquilly : "A soldier I ;
And this strange peace and utter loneliness,
They madden me : nor man nor town is here,
Nor laurels worthy of a warrior's brow ;
And if the promised groves of cinnamon
Be here, we know not—the winds only know !
Nay ! I will back—there's honour in Peru !"
  None moved nor answered, when a distant
     voice
That seemed aerial from the listening wild
Rose syllabled above the forest hum
Articulated humanly, and thrice

In a strange tongue but sweetly kind to hear.

It startled all—save one, whom destiny

With most secure indifference lapped in sleep,

The unconscious owner of the Amazon,

Biding his time.   And first the Father spoke,

Whose spirit, fired with Christian chivalry,

Yearned for adventure in the pagan mind

(And hither on that errand had he come):

" It is the voice of God, spoken by bird

I know not, but believe the omen true.

Inviting was the sound—nay ! let us on !

Speak not of going back : trifles like this,

If it were but the cry of startled bird,

Are trifles only to the heedless ear ;

To those that note them they are proved the
     call

Of Heaven to noble deeds : nay! let us on !

It needs must be that somewhere in these wilds

A remnant of the sundered race of man

In pagan isolation dwells apart

From the great brotherhood, with whom 'tis
     ours

To link them in fraternal bonds of love;
For not alone to us did God's dear Son
Leave the rich legacy of promised Heaven;
And they, the co-heirs with us of His grace,
Wait the announcement privileged to us,
Yea, and enjoined the ambassadors of God
Of His most blessèd embassy to them.
Lofty our mission and our warfare high,
Above the mean ambitions of the flesh,
With demons and the darkened mind : and if,
Pray Heaven it be ! a bloodless victory
Won by the spiritual arm, let the spear rust,
Let Spain be silent of our soundless deeds :
We are the vassals of a higher lord
Of more imperial sway than Charles of Spain !"
    They gave assent, cloaking their secret
        thoughts
Of earthly riches, temporal renown,
With a religious falsehood self-deceived ;
For soon the fair white robe they seemed to
        wear
Of Christianity was splashed with blood,

When, with the fruitless toil renewed in vain,

Exasperate on an Indian tribe they fell

After long search, and, failing in their hopes

Of a sure guide, secured at length though late,

To point their march to El Dorado, used

Torture of steel and fire and hounded dog

On the poor timid wretches to extort

A knowledge from them which they did not
　　know.

What knew they of the dreams in other lands,

Of fancy and unreasoning rumour bred,

That pointed to their own disastrously,

And met a naysay with vindictive rage

And further search infatuate of belief?

Dreams, idle dreams! that haunt the restless
　　mind

With recollection of the primal loss

Of happiness and everlasting youth,

Transferred of old to Heaven's securer clime.

Dreams, idle dreams! worthy alone in this—

They fire the sluggish mind to energy,

Whence spring collateral deeds of lofty strain

That, blindly wrought, in benefits endure
When the false heat that moulded them is cold, ˯
And the unconscious worker, faint and foiled,
Has perished in the flames himself had fanned.

  To kindly nursing in the native tents,
Dumb with the sheer severity of woe,
Gonzalo left his sick, loath to be left,
Not from a fear of vengeance, for their hopes
Swallowed all fear : a godlike fearlessness,
Responsible to none, was in their look,
Which, weakened though they were and
    numbering few,
Struck with paralysis the Indian mind :
But that their eyes should miss the first far
    glimpse
Of unknown empire rising with its towers
Amid the woods and waters onward still,
Whither their comrades with impatient steps
Were certainly advancing.

                    They, meanwhile,
Pushed on through dreary flats of marshy
    land ; —

For the scene changed, and all was desolate :

The forest thinned, and even shrubs were few ;

And, save the plashing of incessant rains

Among the stagnant pools, and the wild cry

Of passing bird lost in the misty air,

With distant winds that round the horizon
  sobbed

Like spirits imprisoned in a drear confine

Searching for freedom, other sound was none ;

Nor did they seek to break the monotone

With show of cheerful talk where cheer was
  none.

And here amid the rainy solitude

A gaunt companion joined them — Famine
  stalked

With fleshless limbs and hollow-staring eyes

Silent beside them, full of brooding thought,

Or chewing bitter buds plucked from dank
  boughs,

Or yellow roots that only bred disease,

From the black soaking soil snatched greedily,

Yet with blue feverish lips mouthed in disgust.

Here sank amid these melancholy wastes,
Like worthless weed, full many an ardent life
Whose value had been left, a cherished hope,
Endeared by many and many a conscious fear
In some particular home, in some one heart,
Hopelessly far in Spain !   And here, perhaps,
They all had perished in a nameless grave,
As some have perished daring deeds as great,
Of whom no record tells, and the stern hum
Of the big drowsy world had sounded on
Unbroken in regardless apathy,
But that the forest with its foodful palms
And medicinal stores opened once more
Its wide asylum to the wasted band ;
And further on beside the Coca's banks
The friendly shelter of an Indian town,
Built underneath one patriarchal roof,
Offered the accepted welcome of a home.
  Long time they tarried here—oh, rest was
    sweet !
And the most ardent of them could have sold
The dowried future, riches, power, renown,

And a salvation from the common blank

On History's glorious page, in glad exchange

For the torn blanket and the garlic meal

Of herdsman on the brownest hills in Spain.

Sickness, fatigue, and fasting, and the sense

Of utter homelessness so tamed their pride,

And they so yearned for human sympathy,

That all mean occupations, once despised,

And all the trammels of society

That gall the fiery spirit to endure,

Seen in their artificiality,

Seen from Brazilian woods afar in Spain,

Were coveted, yea ! realised in dreams ;

Which so subdued their thoughts to humble
   mood

That frankly, when awake, they fraternised

With the meek Indians marvelling much that
   men

Visaged so sadly should have dared so far.

   But with returning health vigour returned,

And the old restlessness stirred in their veins,

And drove them forth a reunited band,

C

Recruited and with fresh access of hope
To penetrate the mystery of the wilds.
The Coca's turbid stream, swollen with the
     rains,
Seemed in their eyes a clew by which to thread
The wilderness : it babbled in their ears
Of distant empire in its lower course
Whither its waters hastened : nay ! it seemed
By very force of sympathy like themselves,
A pioneer peering for hidden lands :
With what mad joy its current leapt along,
Reeling and swaying like a drunk Bacchante,
Startling the temple quiet of the woods
And revelling through their holiest adytum !
Not one of all the Spanish band but threw
A portion of his soul into the stream
And raced with it along : not one but chode
The slow delay, the halts, the tedious turnings
On the swift-rushing river's cumbered banks.
How enviously they saw sweep on before
The speeding fleck of froth, the brittle bell,
Borne on the river's back triumphantly,

Leaving them far behind ! Eagerly now

They would have hurried, having put their hand

Upon the running clew-line of the stream

That promised a safe passage through the dark

Illimitable wild : nearer they seemed

With each day's farther march to friends and
    home,

For they had found a highway to the sea

On whose salt waves no Spaniard could be
    lost.

Yet, as they gazed upon the rolling flood

And with its pace compared their daily march,

Time seemed to stagnate ; and their hopes were
    chilled

With the cold fear, deep-seated in their hearts,

That Fate had caught them in her iron clutch,

Restraining them to a funereal march

Timed to have ending in the desert, where

A sacrificial altar was prepared

On which their hopes should perish, and their
    lives.

Unspoken were their fears ; they even sought,

As brave men will when Fate is at their neck,
To conquer by obedience, to annul
The despotism of dire necessity
By uncomplaining patience, and the show
Of liberty that wears as if in sport
And with a jaunty air a weight of chains.
So from the painful task they turned not back,
Nor paused, nor 'plained, but, though with joy-
    less lips
Flinging upon the air semblance of mirth
In songs that told the glory of the Cid
And ballads of the Moors, right steadfastly
They kept their pensive faces all the while
Fronting the great Unknown.
                The storms were up
One evening when they pitched their wind-
    blown camp
Under the rocking trees beside the stream.
But as they slept o'erwearied with their toil
The tempest sank, and in the sudden calm
A muffled voice came booming up the stream,
Deepening and broadening, a continuous roll

As if of thunder breaking through the folds
Of cloud and night that wrap it seven times
    round,
Until the full-voiced terror drowned the ear
And wrought such horror in the realm of
    dreams
That some from ineffectual struggling woke
Screaming; and others started to their feet
Making the holy sign; and each looked wild
And strangely on his neighbour, gathering in
Slowly his personality of pain.
Never before had European ears
Been so bewildered by such awful noise.
Was Hell broke loose? Or had the keystone
    slipped
That binds the fabric of the bulging globe?
Not even Ordas could conjecture make;
Ordas! who dared the dark volcano's throat
Courting the horrible, what time the flame
Of Cortez' genius shot towards Mexico
Like a clear-burning tongue of arrowy fire
Scorching the dazzling halls of Montezume;

Even Ordas felt a shrinking of the soul,
The veteran Ordas! who in one dark night—
The Night of Sorrows — faced a thousand
    deaths,
Till the last trace of Fear's alloy was purged
From his whole heart for ever.   Day by day
The awful sound with fascinating dread
That drew them towards it, loud and louder
    swelled
Till the wide air was one vast sea of sound,
And from sequestered chambers of the soul
Strange threatening echoes from their primal
    sleep
Rose like a new creation, horrible !
And scarcely was the terror reasoned down
When from the high bank of a river cape
They saw this vast immensity of waters,
Drawn by the Coca from a thousand caves
In the far-distant Andes, leap in mass
Most fearfully into a gulf of air
Two hundred fathoms down : the volumed foam,
That without halt makes everlasting plunge,

Whirled from its sphere of consciousness the
   soul
And left the body, emptied of all feeling,
Tranced in the dumb rigidity of awe.
Nor was their wonder less when farther on
The narrowing torrent with concentred strength
Poured all its length into the channelled rock,
And through the chasm that pent its thun-
   ders in,
A dreadful depth, unsounded of the sun,
Toiled in tumultuous agony : the rocks,
Irrevocably sundered, scowling flung
Defiance on each other front to front,
And heedless of the Hell that howled below.
  On the sheer brink, grasping with knotted
   roots
The stable rock, a giant cedar leaned
Forward, who from the forest had advanced
More dauntless than the rest : him Horror
   seized,
Preventing all return : and on the verge,
Bound in eternal spell, he gazed below.

With ruthless axe assailed, his giant trunk
Fell crashing o'er the chasm from bank to
    bank,
The first beam of a bridge : beside him thrown
Lay lighter palm-trees, in the forest felled :
Gay flowering clusias bound the rolling logs ;
And o'er the airy walk the Spaniards marched,
Horseman and foot, struggling and stumbling
    on,
Till all had passed, safe—to a hostile shore.
For here a shower of darts, blown from the
    woods
Through the long gravatana, sing i' the air,
And hiss and sting !   Anon the ambuscade
With hideous yell advance, a martial race
Accustomed to aggression.   But unknown
To them the sudden flash, the rattling peal
And fatal ravage of the Spanish arm.
Unknown the graceful terror of the steed
That speeds and fights and almost thinks for
    man.
The astonished Indians fled, or grovelling lay

As at the feet of centaurs suppliantly
Conceding all—possessions, children, life.
Under their conduct through a barren tract
The Spaniards journeyed, joyful with the hope
Of rumoured fortune in a distant realm.
And after weary days corn-fields appeared,
And cotton plantings, and the huts of men
Domesticated to a settled life
Arcadian, but with little store of gold.
Here fretting much at their enforced delay
By sickness, hunger, and the present rain—
For now unceasing torrents night and day
Poured from the inky sky, and from its bed
The rising river wandered in gapó,
Flooding the forest—deeming they had reached
The edge of empire where the arts of man
Wage desultory warfare with the wild,
They sent forth pioneers to make survey
For further action : these returning told
Of broken forests, marshes, pools, and ponds,
And squalid tribes inhabiting in trees,
Who yet confirmed, in terror, or in fraud,

The rumoured hints of empire, but remote.

With mingled feelings of despair and hope,

Impatient of suspense, Gonzalo's mind

Resolved a final throw with Fate, which failing,

Farewell the hope that lured him from Quito !

The river was their only highway—smooth

And swift its hurrying waters ran ; it only

Could solve the secret that consumed their soul.

Thus musing in the doorway of his hut

With folded arms, and eyes of brooding gloom

Bent on the muddy flood that tumbled by

Scourged by the slanting rains, the while his
    men

Dozed out the weary moments—musing thus,

Suddenly to his mind a Vision rose,

A fair large vision of a River Ship

That idly lay moored to a bank, with sails

Full-spread and oars, the while the current
    raced

That should have borne the naiad freely on.

Starting, he looked again, and it was gone ;

And th' inscrutable waters whence it rose,

Or seemed to rise, assumed their apathy :
But not less real seemed the gurgling stream
Than that aerial ship that sat the wave,
A moment seen full imaged in the rain,
Then without warning took mysterious flight !
" Saint Jago be my speed," Gonzalo cried,
With spirit roused from her inactive mood,
" And I will make this glorious fiction fact !
Why was I blind to the fair dream till now?
Did not the whispering waters hint of this?
And I, dull schoolboy, understood them not !
Heaven sent me this to fire my flagging
     zeal
In mild reproach : Did not the lively mind
Of Vasco Nuñez on the mountain ridge
Provide a fleet for the yet distant sea?
Dull dreamer that I am ! did not the mules
Of Cortez bear upon their sweltering backs,
O'er many a mile, to launch them in the lakes
Of Mexico, the keels of many a bark?
And I, with a great river in my eyes
Daily, and timber for a sea of ships

In these vast forests where each branching
    trunk
Sends seaward with the rushing winds and
    streams
Its wishes to be free—I saw, I heard it not,
And murmured at my own slow-paced delay!
No more of this! No longer on the banks,
Waiting for fortune, housed in idleness;
But on the river—that way lies my path—
To force her tardy coming!"—In his eyes
The light of genius shone, and where they
    darted
Among his listless followers, a new life
Shot through their veins, and cheerfully re-
    membering
That they had set themselves the task of choice,
Like boys at play they went about the work,
Gonzalo guiding. In the sombrous woods
Screened from the incessant rain and gusty
    winds
That shook and pattered on the slim-built shed
Their workshop in the wild, they built a forge;

And soon the ruddy gleams, forth darting far
Into the cavernous forest, sent their glow
Upon the sinewy limbs and naked breasts
Of willing workers bending at their toil
Or passing to and fro : around the axe
Here thick the splinters flew whitening the
    ground ;
There, as if wakening from its centuried trance
And wakening but to look around and choose
Ground for a resting-place, the stately tree,
Swaying with all its boughs in the high air,
Sank down majestic in its fall, as sinks
Some galleon in mid-ocean in a calm
With sails unfurled and all her bravery on.
Some lop the prostrate branches ; on the stocks
Some stretch the keel, and prop the curving
    frame.
There, half concealed in smoke, a cheerful band
Of demons move, charring the flameless wood
For future fuel : others from the pine,
That stand like patient martyrs ringed with
    fire

Bleeding from many a wound, collect the drops
Of resin as they fall.   One with a box
Makes circuit of the camp, collecting tax
Of ear-rings, finger-rings, crosses, and chains
Of ornamental gold, given willingly,
With armour-plates of silver framed in steel,
And helmets thought superfluous.   In the fur-
    nace
These with the iron shoes wrenched from the
    feet
Of mules and horses, dead or yet alive,
Flung, in the blaze he stands with one arm
    stretched
To stir the glowing coal; the other plies
The groaning bellows.   Like a Cyclops vast
His shadow on a background of green leaves,
Begrimed with smoke, yet glistening in the
    rain,
Toils like a phantom in the noiseless shades
To idle imitation damned.   Anon
The obsidian anvil rings : chief at the work
With sleeves rolled up Gonzalo sweats and toils,

Now at the forge, now swinging the wide axe,
Or straining at a rope, knee touching knee
Familiar with his fellows, bating nought;
And men must follow when their captain bends
The crest of his nobility to toil.

  So from their hands this Argo of the West
Took shape, and grew, and to their houseless
    hopes
Became a very fortress where they sang.
To songs that breathe of ancient chivalry
Opposed to Frank and Moor, in snatches sung,
The unforced product of a hopeful heart
Recalling the achievements of its race,
And in that memory strong—the fair renown
Bernardo heired from brave Orlando slain
At Roncesvalles, or when Gonsalez set
The first stone of Castile; of Vargas, too,
Surnamed the Bruiser, and Ramiro old;
But most of him Spain's matchless paladin
The brave knight of Bivár:—to songs, that
    made
These heroes live in them, the vessel rose,

The structure of their hearts no less than hands,
Endeared by mutual suffering cheerily borne,
For in its sides their hearts were built, and not
Alone their wealth in every driven nail,
Their very clothing steeped in bubbling pitch
Thrust in its seams, and hope of life and home.
Lo ! as they toiled the river-god arose
Curious above his banks, and his great eyes
Gleamed through the trees upon them at their
     toil ;
Then, as if found the object of his quest,
The virgin vessel, with tumultuous rush
He flung out his long arms, folding her round,
And like a bridegroom took her to his breast.

    And now, their more immediate wishes met,
The dull reaction came with idle hands
Of labour wasted : what were one small bark
Where scarcely forty would suffice to bear
Their numerous band along?   The greater
     part,
With futile efforts every hour renewed,
Hewed for themselves along the bosky banks

Their woodland way, while in the brigantine
A scanty complement of sickly men
Waited, with oars backed in the hurrying rush
Of the impetuous stream, the slow-paced march
Of their o'erwearied comrades on the shore.
So passed laborious weeks, till hunger-forced,
And tempted by fresh rumours of a land
Rich in all blessings—food, and towns, and
    gold,
Far down the river where a mightier stream
Engulfed the Coca, they made general halt
Arguing the folly of the bridled ship,
On the free element a captive log,
Bound to the sluggish measures of the land.

D

BOOK II.

By this the happy season was returned
When to the texture of his cloud-built tent
Diaphanous the red-faced sun approached,
Peering into the shrouded world below
That languished in the rain : the curtains
    caught
The glory of his burning countenance
And went ablaze : this way and that they fled,
And lo ! the lofty firmament serene
In a wide stretch of deep ethereal blue
Enroofed the laughing globe. There hung the
    sun ;
And Nature stretched her praiseful arms aloft
In distant hills and towering trees and waves

And little humble flowers adoringly
Towards the benignant Sun, that smiled again !
Along the forest glades now might you see
The wavering flight of indolent butterflies
Whose blue metallic wings lit up the shades
Like fluttering patches of the fallen sky.
The yellow troupials whisked from bank to
    bank,
And hung their pendent nests on the high
    boughs
That swayed in graceful fringes down the sky.
While ever and anon the frigate-bird
With head thrown back came sailing down the
    air
That streamed above the stream, and dis-
  . appeared.
Ah me ! what wistful faces sad and wan
And wasted with disease met the red gaze
Of the returning sun !   How with the heavens
Their prisoned hopes enlarged, defying bounds,
Yet chafing at the strange mysterious leash
That pulled them to the wingless body back.

Meanwhile as if from sudden ambush sprang
A lurking fever on the pallid frame
Of stout Gonzalo : from his restless couch
He turned his hungry eyes upon the priest :
—"O holy father, must I here abandon,
Here within promised access of renown,
The great hope of my days? And must I die,
Thus circumstanced with new-awaking life
In all around me? Water, earth, and air,
The winds, the sunbeams, insect, bird, and river
Rejoice unfettered : I am captive bound.
Oh for the pinions of yon passing bird,
That I at least might overfly the land,
And, if but with a transient glimpse, drink in
The wealth of my possessions! Hard it is
To be the heir of what I cannot hold ;
Harder, indeed, if I have brought you all
Into this sylvan solitude, apart
From human ken, only to waste and die
In unrecorded pain! And therefore I
Would send at least, if that I may not go,
To claim my heritage : call Orellana!

I have marked him fit for noble deeds,
Approved him bold, ay, somewhat over-bold,
And think him true.   What if the after-race
Ignoring or in ignorance credit *him*
With all the honour of the enterprise !
I shall not mind it, though it cut me now
Even to anticipate.   Vain fear ! 'tis *mine;*
Nor have I less the greatness that I feel
Wanting the confirmation of the crowd."

"A noble deed," gravely the priest replied,
" Done in obscurity or deepest night,
Needs not the shouting of the multitude
To make it fact,—yea ! and if but conceived
When other hands receive it at the birth,
Stolen or adopted, none the less remains
In highest truth the author's.   A brave mind,
Strong in the consciousness of native worth
As hero in his mail, will estimate
The praise of men as but a needless cloak
Thrown over armour :   And yet true it is
The purple trappings and the nodding plume
Become the warrior well ;—but they are less

His own delight than worn to pleasure friends.

Think you the great Columbus, when the light

First showed him where the long-lost hemi-
sphere

Lay sleeping in the void—think you he felt

At that abandoned hour of soundless night

Less sure of his own greatness, as he stood

On the lone poop surrounded by the dark

While Europe far behind in her grey walls

Chaffered and gossiped through her daily
rounds

Forgetful of him quite, or mindful only

As of a fond enthusiast pitiable—

Than when, after long months of secret greatness,

He told to courts his prophecy fulfilled,

And Europe, pausing in her mill-horse round,

Turned all her million eyes to the grey seas,

The riddle of whose mystery was read,

And hailed him Finder of a Second World?

And yet, when all is said, be sure his mind

Chose her seat well,—not on the unstable base

Of airy speech of men, which a side wind
Blowing sinister with capricious gust
Can sweep as swift away as castled clouds
Before an evening gale,—not on renown
As men translate the word, an empty sound,
Which themselves give and often give awry,
And then withhold, and with as little cause ;
But on the steadfast rock, the immortal stance
Of consciousness of a great duty done.
In that one word all honest greatness hides,
And each may grasp it in his several sphere,
For that is duty that a man can do
And that beseems a man—all else is vain."
He ended, but the germinating thought
Grew in Gonzalo's mind.   Upon the priest
His large eyes gazed in silence till his mind,
Slow to appropriate the strength-giving truth,
Returned the dictum like a lingering echo—
"Yea ! that is duty that a man can do,
And mine is now to send, not mine the event,
Since that I may not go : call Orellana !"—

    A young man still, though in his auburn hair

Time's silvery threads were spreading, and his
  brow
Had gathered more than one long line of grey.
But in his eye the wandering light of youth
Still showed a mind unsettled in its aim,
Though powerful to achieve what others
  planned.
A dreamer was he in his hours of ease,
And careless of preferment undeserved
By action of his own. A volunteer,
He came from drowsing by the torpid banks
Of Guadiana to the Western world,
Smit with the hope of some great deed of
  fame,—
Which so absorbed his soul that lesser gain
For its own sake, or as a central germ
That tarries the slow-fostering of the years,
Was blown contemptuous to the passing winds;
For he would be at once i' the eye o' the world,
Or live and die among the shadows seen
By none. Yet think not he was idle all,
Waiting to strike and strike but once for fame :

His sword was ever at his chief's command,

And what he undertook his very daring

And utter recklessness, or rather say

Firm confidence of the event, made sure and
    fast

A fact in history. But mark his pride

Or self-neglect, or call it what you will

—After such enterprise he shunned to meet

His grateful leader; and his comrades' praise

Around the barrack-fire or in the tent,

In town or field, fell cold upon his ear :

Upon his heel he turned, and, listlessly

Reclining on his couch with half-shut eyes,

Or roaming vacantly in lonely places,

They found him, and gave up the thankless task.

Or if importunate the public voice

Threatened ovation—he would seize his cloak ;

His sword was ever belted to his side ;

And disappear. Thus had he joined the band

A day's march late that journeyed from Quito

Under Gonzalo. Thus he clipt the winglets

Of his own growing fame; for he would soar

At once i' the eye o' the world, or sink unseen
Among the shadows, known to none or all.
—" If I have sent for thee," Gonzalo said,
" 'Tis not to speak thy praise; for what thou
  hast
Deserving praise thou hast from Heaven, and
  there
The honour lies; and that thou knowest un-
  moved
By voice of man ; and therefore praise is thine
In that I choose thee from among the rest,
Deeming thee loyal, who hast well approved
The motive of thy acts, to take my place
And duteously fulfil my vows to Spain
And to my brother : thou shalt take command
Of this our ark, the brigantine—that bears
The fortunes of our expedition : I
Commit them to thy charge. Do thou descend
Whither the Indians tell.   Of some great
  stream
That rolls its ink and flings its yellow foam
Around some central capital they tell.

There glory waits thee, ripened to thy hook;
But bring me back a sheaf—a few stray ears
I surely well may claim !   We tarry here.
Our hopes, our very life goes with thee !   See
Thou prove no alien !   Choose thy men, and
    go !"—

   And Orellana knelt, and kissed the hand
Of great Gonzalo, rose, and nothing said
But turned in act to go.   With searching eyes
Gonzalo gazed upon his soldier bearing
As wishful for some proof of loyalty ;
Then, as it came not, turning to the priest—
" Thou, too," he said, " wilt go."—" Nay, here I
    stay,"
The father answered ; "tempt me not, my son,
With the fruition of an earthly fame
Bought with a bartered conscience !   Even now
The Devil is at mine elbow—I can feel
His fingers on my shoulder, in mine ear
His hot breath urging me to make a league
With him and thee and Heaven; take thine
    offer,

Abandon thee with all the show of friendship,

Compound with Heaven for a brief course of
    sin

By future sanctity—the greater saint

And more acceptable to heaven the more

I give my passions rein !   ' And what is he ?

A sick man dying in the wilderness,

A withered stalk upon the tree of life

That will be green no more'—Satan, avaunt !

And thou, Gonzalo !—these are devil's words

That urge my going, put into thy mouth

By thy great enemy and mine and man's :

Speak them no more !   For, grant I leave thee
    here

And go to what great glories who can doubt,

How shall I hear and see amid the glare

And blaze of triumph the dispassionate voice

And the white star of duty? till perchance

The tumult has sunk down and the time gone

For doing duty?   Oh, the Devil ever

Wraps round a man the mantle of his praise

Spoke by the yelling multitudes, whene'er

He means to hide the irrevocable chance
Of a great duty offered by the Lord !—
So tempt me not !"

              The words were vehement
And uttered as in anger—eyeballs starting,
And the full veins upon his beaded brow
Relieved like whipcord. From his pillow raised
Upon one elbow, breathless, pallid, fixed
As stares a statue with its marble eyes
Rounded with wonder, and with doubt con-
      gealed,
Gonzalo gazed upon the speaker. In
The hush that followed a cicala ran
Across the open doorway, on the roof
Outside the tapping of a woodpecker
Was heard, and one low distant moan subdued
Its anguish in the woods. The father's eye
Fell, and a chill ran through his frame : " For-
      give,"
He said, in a strange wearied tone
Altered and low : " Forgive the unwonted heat ;
For thou know'st not, my son, the carnal heart

That beats beneath this mantle, as do I !"
   Sudden, and at a bound, Gonzalo leapt
From his sick-bed, and with a strong man's
      voice—
" What guarantee have I, if thus the storms
Of wild ambition shake the Holy Church
Personified in thee—what proof have I
That Orellana will not play me false,
Self-duped in sending him?   Go! call him
      back !
I, I myself—Here by sheer strength of will
I fling this fever from me !—It is mine ;
The glory I have traced to this far haunt
No hand shall seize but mine!   And bring my
      mail—
I, I myself will head the enterprise.
No proxy suits with me.   This very hour—
Nay, on the instant—stand aside !"
                              For here
The father caught him staggering to the door,
And forced him back, panting and flushed and
      faint

Upon the couch. " Dost thou withstand me?"
  " I
Withstand thee not—it is the hand of Heaven !
Is this the resignation thou didst feel?
Such resignation is but the result
Of weakness to rebel.   If thou wouldst live
And heir the honour Heaven intends for thee
Obey me !"—for he struggled yet to rise.
" I have hid nothing from thee.   Therein lies
My error : but that I am true to thee
Believe, and let me show it by remaining.
Ask me no more to go : I will not go !
My duty is with thee—and with these others,
Our numerous sick, that must remain behind ;
But chief with thee; for thou art marked by
      Heaven
For some great work, and I have charge of
      thee !
Only live thou to do it.   It is thine
If one go at thy bidding though thy hand
Should never finger the dictated work ;
And that a servant here relieve thy hand

The hand of God upon thee laid in sickness
Gives clear assurance 'tis the will of Heaven.
—As for this Orellana, let him go
Since one must go and thou hast chosen him !
And for those fierce temptations that in thought
Assailed my soul a short while since—of this
Be sure, no fiercer storm, no tempest half so
    fierce
Can Satan raise in Orellana : ' I,'
(Thou say'st; for I can read thy inmost thoughts,
Knowing my own so well) 'If I,' thou say'st,
' A son of Holy Church can be so tempted,—
If I a green branch burn so fiercely, what
Swift - tongued destruction must lick up the
    dry ? '
—Am I a green branch ?   I have read my life
And studied my whole nature : that I am
A son of Holy Church I know, and boast,
Unworthy though I be ; but Holy Church
Gives not a change of nature : I have here
Under these pious vestments the wild pulse
Of warrior, and—root out the infirmity,

O Heaven !—I feel a tigerish instinct stir
Even in the pastoral service of the Church
If bloodshed would but frighten to the fold
The heathen flocks that roam the wilderness !
To thee I make confession of my weakness
That this confession may be as a chain
To bind me closer to thee ! I believe
That in our band no breast is visited
With half so fierce temptations, nor no heart
Half so susceptible of earthly fame !
And thou mightst but commission me to ruin,
To send me girt with equal power with him
This tool, this Orellana, whose dull heart,
Though stout to dare what others planned, was
    never
Stirred with the nobler passion to create
And carve self-confident for his own ends.
Fear not; this tool will do the work for thee
More faithfully than I thy truer friend,
And I shall yet be saved for thee and Heaven ! "

    More was there in his looks and in his tone
Than in the words, uttered impulsively

E

And wildly ordered, to assure Gonzalo
The revelation was indeed sincere.
He stretched him out his hand ; quickly the
  priest
As catching at salvation caught the grasp
Ere yet half way, and held it tight and long.
Gonzalo's generous heart returned the pressure,
And " I have known thee long," he said ; "but
  never
Known truly till this hour. With reckless hand
Thou hast loosened for me a prop on which
I leaned as on a hill—nay ! hear me out ;
There need be now no secrets 'twixt us twain :
For I had thought thee steadfast as the Earth,
Infallible as Heaven : Thou art, instead,
Even in thy weaknesses, thy doubts of self,
Thy struggles with the flesh, and all thy fears,
A brother on whose breast I yet may lean,
If not with such security as once,
Surely with a new sympathy that both
Imparts and gathers strength. And so, I trust
  thee ;

Go he, stay thou, thy will is wholly mine!"

    While yet he spake Day fell; the sunset spilt
Its crimson on the waters; down the stream
With a great rush it sped, purpling the wood,
The river-banks, the brigantine, the air,
With the reflection of its sanguine glow.
It was a world of red—red leaves, red waves,
Red faces; e'en Gonzalo's pallid face
Took on the hue of health: all things were
    dyed
In the rich rubious translucent streams
Of the great fountain welling in the West!

    The Father's eyes were on Gonzalo, his
Looked wistfully out through the open door
Of the rough wooden shed—his hospital—
Upon the evening glory of the world:
The brigantine lay moored within his gaze
Motionless, save where the eye might note
A certain rhythmic movement of her mast
Obedient to the lapping of the stream.
What thoughts were his, what longings or what
    fears,

He uttered not, save that unconsciously
By pressure of the hand fast locked in his
He intimated to the watchful priest
A spirit busy within him forcing up
The gateways of the future. Thus they sat,
The Father with his broad back towards the
      door
Shrouded in shadow. On Gonzalo's face
The red light died away, the air grew dim ;
Wild dissonant cries answering to dissonant
      cries
Of birds and chattering apes, unearthly screams !
Ran like a desecration down the aisles
Of the wide-vaulted wood. Low in the shade,
Appearing here and reappearing there,
Tiny initial sparks of wavering fire
Twinkled about, till o'er the tufted trees
Diana raised her argent arc and shot
The first dart of her beauty through the gloom !
   The solemn Night was hers : high o'er the
      woods
That underneath spread like a sea of leaves,

O'er which the night-wind moaned and made
  no stir
Among the billows and reposeful waves,
She walked serene in chosen loneliness
As if her meditations would outlast
Eternity. The wanderers were asleep
Wrapt in oblivious visions all, save one,
The holy Father : He, from where he sat,
Beside Gonzalo's couch, gently unclasped
The sleeper's feverish hand, and gathering up
The rustlings of his robe, stole from the shed
With more than woman's care. At the low
  door
Free from the shadow of the shed he stood
Full in the moonlight. First he glanced to
  heaven,
Then on the width of waters weltering by
Fixed his keen gaze as if he would enforce
Confession of the secret of their goal :
More stealthily the waters seemed to glide
Under his searching eye ; and longer he,
Rapt in a reverie of human life,

The mystery of its birth and course and end,
Had stood, entranced under the mystic spell
Of moonlight on a river yet unnamed
Lying familiarly, but that a fish
Leapt up the stream and sank with peaceful
plunge
Amid a spray of diamonds ; whereat
The Father started, brushed the dreams away
With open hand across his troubled brow,
Then with uplifted face looked straight to
heaven,
The silver moonlight on his moving lips
As if in prayer : from the pure deeps above
That from the feet of God flow down to earth
His spirit drank assurance, rest, and faith,
And was refreshed.
Along the river-bank
He passed to where the watch half leaned, half
lay
Snoring against a tree : his head thrown back
Revealed his naked throat that glimmered white
Beneath a beard black-pointed toward the moon.

With angry hand he twitched the sleeper's
    beard—

" Rouse thee ! but question not — where lies
    to-night

Young Sanchez?" And the sentinel abashed,

Awkward, and dazed, with spear-encumbered
    hand

Rubbing his chin, glanced wildly round the
    camp,

Then pointing with the other—" Near the bank

In the big tent beside the tall assaí :

'Tis he relieves me." " Let him relieve thee
    now !

If I mistake not, thou art one of those

Impatient of preferment, and unfit

To fill the meanest post with the first want,

Fidelity : go, house thee in a sheet ;

And when—for fate gives sloth a length of
    years—

They ask thee to recount at home in Spain

The achievements of thy youth, boast of thy
    deeds,

But in thy boasting, blush to recollect
This night's disgrace !   Comrade ! take this,
    and go—
A year of loyal service, borne with pain,
And left to speak its own reward, will scarce
Efface the blot upon thy name to-night ! "

    Came from beneath a tall paxinba's roots,
That as on tiptoe stood stretching its neck
Above its forest *confrères*, Hernan Sanchez,
Equipped   for   outpost   duty.   Straight   he
    marched
And steady as a tower to where the priest
Waited his coming : "Art thou one," said he,
" Of Orellana's band ? "   The soldier bowed—
" One of the fifty I."   " A volunteer ? "
" Sought   out," replied the youth with modest
    pride,
" Ere yet I knew to intercede to go ! "
" Thou art Gonzalo's standard-bearer ? "   "Yea ;
By his own gift that honour do I bear ! "
" And he has honoured thee ! requite it, youth !
—Tell me, for youth has still a live ideal

By which to dress its conduct, who is thine?"

"The Marquis, ere we left Quitó; since then,

Oh, need'st thou ask? our noble chief Gonzalo."

"Thou art not one of those who worship still

The rising star?" "Thou wouldst insult me,
  priest?

—Prove me, and then upbraid me!" "Nobly
  said;

'Tis for that end I come, to prove and—praise
  thee!

For when thy conscience, speaking in thy breast,

Shall praise thy conduct, hear in it the voice

Of honest men; among which rank am I,

And own no other. Thou wilt go to-morrow

Under the leadership of Orellana

To great discoveries, freedom, life, and fame.

Let not the whirl of fortune turn thy head:

Remember thou thy fealty to Gonzalo;

He goes with you—misunderstand me not—

For Orellana is but as thyself,

Nor more nor less, divested of the power

Lent him by great Gonzalo: honour it,

Be jealous of it in thy leader's charge ;
But see thou make no transfer of thy faith
To him the man that wields it !—I had said
The same to Orellana following thee
Hadst thou been chosen to the chief command.
There is no treason in my counsel, then,
But truest loyalty to those that go
And those that stay : we constitute a State
Commissioning you with powers which you
　　　may use
Against the State that grants them. This he
　　　knows,
This Orellana ; and I have no cause
To doubt his faithfulness : assist him, thou,
To keep his faith—but slay him if he fail !"

　　This said, abrupt he turned and disappeared
Back to his post in the low wooden shed
Where in delirious sleep Gonzalo lay
Tossing.
　　　　　　The camp next morning was astir
As dawn crept up the water : with the first
Long level lance of pioneering light

That struck the tall paxinba's topmost plume
Ten thousand voices woke, and the dim wood
And the grey air burst from the trance of Night;
And screams and shrieks and sharp dissevered
    notes
That intimated freedom rent the sky.
Flocks of white, green, and scarlet parroquets
Leapt from their perch; thousands of toucans
    flew
With outstretched bill seeking their morning
    meal :
Here on a heavy-podded inga's branch
Some twenty would alight with clumsy foot,
Shaking the ripe fruit ready for the drop
Into the stream a hundred feet below :
The nimble trogon with obedient wing
Skimming the mid-air, swerved with easy grace
And caught the falling fruit and disappeared.
Herons, and terns, and gulls innumerable
Followed the sinuous current, or made halt
Upon a floating tree, or on the marge
Searched for their food among the water-weeds.

While ever and again a kingfisher,
With back of glossy green, shot down the river
Like volant ball; and golden orioles,
And troupials, banded black and yellow,
    whisked
From nest to mid-air and from mid-air back
To slender purse-like nest depending fair
From the high branches all adown the sky.
Amid the lower shrubs that fringed the strip
Between the wood and water, bush-shrikes ran,
Their long loose silky feathers fluttering fierce
With joy, as they impaled with corneous beak
Their insect-victims on the hard-barked bough.
Meanwhile the golden disc of the new sun
Shone through the trees like a great shield of
    gold :
Whereat the moon grew faint, and stole away
Worn to transparent thinness in the West ;
And as the round of red rejoicing Day
Rose free at last of forest-screen, she slipped
Ghost-like behind the shelter of the hills.
    How do familiar scenes, daily beheld,

And daily held to be the stereotype
Of long-traditioned nature meaning nothing,
Grow suddenly significant ! What power,
Ebbing and flowing in the speechless air,
And growing half-articulate in the cries
Of birds, and in the whispers of the woods,
And smiling in the sun, or in the cloud
Frowning, gives character and mood and mind
To dull or idle nature?—Nay, what power
In man informs the brutish earth with soul,
Shooting a meaning into clods and stones
To prop a hope or feed a cherished fear?
'Tis not in nature : but the God in man,
As man was God-created from the clay,
Breathes into nature mystery of meaning,
Then wrests her riddle to his own desire,
Strengthened and propped by natural sympathy.
So to the nobler of that hopeful band
Whom Orellana gathered to his cause
Came with a speedier course that morning's sun,
And larger life was on the water's marge
Pulsing with warmer flow in every wing.

Nature expectant of a famous deed
That day should see commence was earlier up.
In all they saw there was a harmony
Benevolent to their purpose, and the heavens
Smiled in consent of all their hopes and
    schemes.

Under the smiling morn the patient bark
Slept idly on the shallows : hasty feet
Struck heavily on the gangway—a slim plank
That swung from shore to ship; but still she
    dreamed
Rocked in the eddying waters : fruit sun-dried
And mandioc meal in bags and boxes borne
On willing backs were hurried up the plank
And tumbled in the vessel: with more heed
Guns, and gunpowder in a chest ill spared
From a diminished stock, were stored ; and
    now
A hasty meal was snatched or from the stream
By flowering thorn-hook, or from sweet assaí
In clusters of small purple berries struck
By climber with his pole : then came the priest

And in the ears of all confirmed the charge
Of Orellana, limiting his power,
And asking his acceptance of the trust
In words which Orellana gave,—and gave
Besides fealty in clear well-ordered phrase
Both for himself and men to great Gonzalo.
Thus satisfied the Father caused advance
The leader and his fifty from the rest ;
And while they knelt, dinting the forest spores
And choking many a weedy cassia's bells
And flowered convolvulus, around the priest,
He solemnised promise and enterprise
By special mass appointed by the Church
For mariners at sea, and shrived them all.

    The ritual o'er, like schoolboys freed from
      school
They raced on board the galley, swung her
      round
Instinct with life into the middle channel
Churning the stream. ere scarce the tense-
      drawn rope
That kept her to her moorings snapt across

And curling sprayed the water. Then like bird
Hovering in mid-air on vibrating pens
Ere yet it flies a straight course down the gale,
She, quivering with the sudden keen delight
Of freedom, all her dreams shook to the air,
A moment with backed oars stood on the
 stream,
Then, thrusting out like one her twenty paddles,
Dipped with a thought in the thin element,
And bounded forth between her lines of foam,
That widened in her wake, and waned away
Amongst the tumbling river ere the cheer
Of God-speed ! from their comrades on the
 bank
Ceased in the rowers' ears. Their answering
 hail
Came back as from another world, faint-voiced
And far and past recall. And long they gazed
Ranged on the bank like statues of despair
Staring with strained and film-o'erspreading
 eye
After a disappearing hope : they saw

Rise on the bark now dwindled to a bird
The white wing of her sail ; and as the curve
Of wooded shore denied them farther view
It made partial amends by sending back
An echo of the boat-song sifted drear
Through the dim arches of the pillared palms.
   Sank from the light and life of cheerful day
The lingering echoes falling restfully
Into the caves of silence,—as distil
Through chinks and cracks to intramontane
    wells
The drops which twinkled on the tempest's
    wing
In rainbow lustre ere the tumult rose
That dashed them with a myriad diamonds
    more
Into the surging heather ! Sank the strain
From healthful morn : yet through the curtain
    door
Which severs dreamland and the drear abode
Of shadows from the light of open day
A thrice-enfeebled wail ran plaintively :

F

It crossed Gonzalo's spirit in the dark,
Labouring belated like a lonely bird
Above a moaning sea through cloud and storm
And falling stars and ruin and eclipse;
And in his sleep wrought on mysteriously
The patient tossed his arms in weak despair.

The bark shot onward into unknown scenes.
So shot the ray of new-created light
Into chaotic gloom: so bursts the dawn
Of knowledge on the wondering infant mind.
Chaos, surprised with happiness, looked grim,
Laughed, and danced into cosmic loveliness:
Even so the mind breaks into rapturous singing
And leaps with joy of an immortal pulse.
And did not the new scenes laugh and look
    glad,
And shape their gladness into dance and song,
To be thus visited and viewed of man,
Far wandering but arrived at last, though late,
To claim his due inheritance?

                The river
Proud of the burden bore the heirs along

Of all the Amazons, sang at the prow
The songs of hope, and at the helm repeated
The achievements of the past in choral praise.
The little waves that sparkled in the sun,
And smiled, and ran hand linked in tiny hand,
Gay messengers transmitted from the bows,
Lisped to the crowded banks, and venturous
    reeds
Advanced to meet them in the shallow bays,
"The long-expected heirs are passing by."
Whereat the rushes waved their bannerets
And the bright banks broke into brighter bloom.
The forest formed its ranks along the shores
And crowded forward, where the river bent,
With homage and oblation long delayed
But now extended in each laden bough.
The very airs, the wandering spies of heaven,
That roam from Alp to Andes, seeing all
Man's glories and the grandeur of the world,
Caught the contagious glow of sympathy
With wave and wood, and whispered flattering
    tales.

The homage and the tribute and the triumph
Were seen and felt by all as with one heart.
For as the hours fled and the distance grew
Between them and their comrades left behind
They gathered in, mutely, by slow degrees
Community of feeling, hopes and fears,
That merged at last incorporate in the bark
Into identity.   Thus animate
Forward they sped with ever-joyful leaps
Along the reaches of the mighty stream.
Suns rose and set paving their level path
With robes of scarlet and with cloth of gold.
Night flung submissive at their fearless feet
Her gemmed tiaras and her strings of stars,
The dowry of old Time : the silver moon
From a full horn rained tribute down the sky
And widened nightly in admiring wonder,
While still the attendant winds buzzed flatter-
        ingly
Of marvels that should open on their view,
And willingly gave up their wonted freedom
To guide and retinue the sons of Spain

Through valley lands long centuries known to
   them.

On swept the brig borne on the river's back,

While hopes like cherubim flew on before,

Their white wings rustling ever round the bows

Or ever disappearing in a flash

Of dazzling plumes at every vista's end

Or shady turning !   On—no need for pause :

The river gave them of its watery stores ;

The trees held out their fruitage, and they
   plucked

With unstayed course, sparingly, as they passed

The offered bounty of the burdened bough.

It was the noon of Night : a far-off moon

Looked from the lofty firmament aslant

Down on the speeding brigantine through twists

Of stationary cloud.   The winds blew soft,

Rocking the slumb'rous trees ; and all was
   still,—

Save where the forest-hum for ever in

Incipient burst of speech deceived the listener ;

And there was, too, the babble and the throb
Of lapsing waters felt along her keel
Lifting the vessel, as a cross is lifted
Gently upon the bosom of a nun
Inhaling and exhaling in her dreams
Regular breath.   The helmsman at his post
Dreamt of Castile.   High on the forward deck
Stood one whose brow the moon with cooling
    beams
Tiara'd,—while with sleepless glance he ques-
    tioned
His future of the stars :
                    " Say ye who stand
A scriptured mystery on creation's wall,
Revealed by night, invisible in the sun,—
If in your radiance wrapt from human ken,
As ye are wrapt in all-unfolding Day,
The story of my destiny is traced !
And I may know but that I may fulfil
With firmer, bolder heart Heaven's hopes in
    me!   .   .   .
  " Faith in myself I have not : I am but

A waif upon the tide of human life,

Helmed and commanded by a higher power,

Whose fingers on my fate I seem to feel

Shaping my course, and leaving me,—as I

Shape for this passive brig its unknown way

At intervals upon the drifting stream. . . .

   " Let me indulge the fancy : ships there are

That rule the waves awhile : there waits for
     them

A smiling surface and a hidden rock.

Some, with contemptuous gesture tossed to
     land

A broken wreck, waste publicly away.

Others the ocean slips from, leaving them

Upon a barren beach, their ventures o'er,

Henceforth to blister in the sun, and rot.

—Each has its various end.—But who would
     see

In all the necessary whirls and shifts

Of fortune that befall or floating logs

Or floating ships the hand of God, save him

Who gives his god indeed impossible power

But less of wisdom than himself to guide it? . . .

"Chance rules it all; or else the fool is right
Who, rather than seek out with patient search
The mighty Maker, makes one for himself
And worships his own idol—not less surely
Than blacks in Africa their wooden blocks;
—Worships a baby god who takes delight
In dropping nuts into a forest pool
To hear the lonely splash, in whirling logs
Along the barren seas, and puffing leaves
Rustling and red around an idle hill. . . .

"And may not man, superior though he be,
To whom with nuts and logs and leaves the
    same
Final decay succeeds an idle life,
Be equally the abandoned toy of chance
And orphaned of his Maker? . . .

                              "'Tis not so
With him: inferior nature, to itself
Left and the governance of man, repeats
Its patient function ordered from without
Incapable of will; but man is free,

Though, still partaking of the lumpishness
Of mortal earth, he be the slave of law
So far; and may be wholly; to the which
His grosser nature drags him, drugs his will,
And wraps the aspiring spirit flesh-encased
In most ignoble slothfulness and sleep.
But souls of noble possibility,
Though lapped in indolence, shall rouse at last
And will their liberty and laugh at law.
Among which rank am I; no more a boat
Beached among shells and shingle, or afloat
Upon a drifting current idly borne
Helmless, and having no far haven marked,
Its free-determined aim, beyond the roar
Of surges and cyclones, and past the maze
Of atoll, archipelago, and shoal.

    "'Tis flow-tide with me, and I feel the chance
That has withdrawn its strong sustaining waves
From underneath Pizarro's stranded bows
Lapping my fortunes and upbearing me.
But here I ask no more, would trust no more
To idle chance, but, master of my will,

Wrest from the laws of gross inferior earth
My future, and contrive with strenuous care
Of my own choice a famous destiny. . . .

　Would Heaven but give assurance of my wish
And of my hope, confirming them to faith
That I am free and master of myself,
How would the token I entreat in vain
Nerve me with triple strength to bend the laws
Of nature to my will!　I have been long
A very tool to other men, with which
They smote to their own purposes the chains
Which nature would impose; then flung me by,
A disregarded and inglorious—fool.

　"Enough of this!　Hereafter for myself
I work—I plan, I live, I joy in freedom!
Chance favours me; Nature, already tamed,
Turns with obsequious smile her sympathy
Upon me; and the stars—if ever stars
Registered in their rubric on Heaven's door
A lofty deed, may have some trace of mine.
Never,—if in obedience to the priest
I, backward toiling, bear my own deserts

And fling them at the feet of a Pizarro
Disburdening me of glory all my own.
But verily if onward on this highway,
Which ends indeed at Charles's throne in Spain !
The question is—backward or forward, then :
Back to obscurity, to keep my faith
With one who robs me of the fame I win ;
Onward to fame and freedom, life and power,
—And ignominy of a broken word
And an abandoned friend ? "

          He paused, and weighed
The question, while his hand balanced a sword
Mechanically mimicking his mind.
" Give sign, ye stars,
Ye voiceless keepers of Heaven's closed ar-
    chives,
That hold his former and his latter will !
Say, is it Heaven's great will that having had
The reins of this behemoth-river thrust
Into my hands, I fling them in the air
To the wild hands of hundreds stretched to
    grasp them ;

Or that I bridle him through all his bounds
And ride him to the sea?"

                    Just then a star
By unseen fingers lightly disengaged
Slid from the zenith in a line of light,
That was reflected in the river's course,
Eastward o'er hidden empire to the sea.
It fell into the scale-pan of the balance
That symbolled progress in the thoughtful mind
Of Orellana : doubt, distrust of self,
Loyalty, and danger, and delay and fear
Flew up and kicked the beam.

                    " Be this," he cried
With arm upraised, "the signal that I seek !
It woos me down the water ; in its flight
It sped like arrow from the bow of Heaven
Shot o'er the region that I yet shall rule
To guide me to my kingdom !—'Tis enough !
There is no wrong in following Heaven's decree,
There is no faltering fear : Heaven's eyes be-
    hold
Me, and my hopes are histories in Heaven !"

The steersman Sanchez, dreaming o'er the
    helm
Of tranquil ease and household joys obscure
Afar in fair Castile, roused by the words,
Looked up to see his leader on the poop
Transfigured in the moonlight, falling clear
Of cloud or bough around him, by resolve
To something more than seems in common
    man.

On o'er the olive pathway of the stream
Through solitudes lit up with radiant suns
Or steeped in mystic moonlight, joyfully
With song upon their lips or lapped in dream
Calmly they glided, trusting in the calm
Reliant face of their still-thoughted leader.
One day at noon, rounding a river cape
Clothed with a lofty forest, ere they knew
They slid into a black tumultuous stream
Of broken waves that hurrying from the West
Made sudden swerve to southward, drinking
    swift

In its fierce wrath the placid olive wave,
And swirling the frail bark caught in the rapids
Round in the yellow foam. By dexterous twist
Of rudder aided by auxiliar oar
They shot into still water, and lay to
Upon a sandy bottom on the lee
Of a large island where in former years
The rivers mingling met,—now far below.
And here they landing looked in vain for tower,
Temple, or teocalli o'er the waste
Of woodland stretching round—listened in vain
For cymbal or for drum where in far glades
Or on sequestered plains religious rites
Might then be celebrating, or great chiefs
Or borla'd monarch holding with his queen
Peaceful review or mustering troops for war.
And here they fell in passionate dispute
Of farther action, frequently renewed,
Yet ever ending in divisive taunt
And more divisive silence. To go back
Now that the goal was reached were to preserve
The faith of gentlemen. This was opposed,—

It were the work of months against the stream

Toiling, and even if the work were done

What could it bring Gonzalo or themselves

But disappointment of a fostered hope

Of fame to him; to them the mute reproach,

Loud-tongued perchance, of disappointed men?

Then to go forward—that were breach of faith,

Shameful desertion of confiding friends

And blindfold rush through danger;—or it
were

Bravery, and reason, and a sure reward.

And so they strove, through the long hours of
noon,

With the strange Stygian river's dismal hue,

That would receive no glory from the sun,

Reflected in their faces. In the gaps

And pauses of their talk, one heard the note

Of drowsy bell-bird, snow-white o'er the shade

Of mountain-forest faint and far away.

At length up sprang the leader: he had
watched

With vigilant eye the varying tide of talk,

And now broke silence. "In this camp," he
    said,

" There are two parties where there should be
    one.

—One in the brig, while I command her, one

And only one there must be ! " Here he paused,

Then with his scabbard on the firm smooth
    sand

He drew a parting line : " You that believe

I should command that party, cross this line

And range yourselves beside me : here stand
    I ! "

And stepped across with sword unsheathed.
    Many

With acclamation leapt across the line ;

Some crossed in silence; and, with lingering
    step,

Others ; till only one at last remained,

Young Sanchez.   Him the sole inhabitant

And prisoner of a melancholy isle

They left, his brave face turned from them
    away

Proudly resentful of their mocks and prayers,

And loyal to Gonzalo.   Off they fled

Like unreturning arrow swiftly loosed

From a strong bow new bent.   Free was their
  course

Upon the hurrying rapids down the stream,

Yet aided still by twinkling oar, and sail

Hoised on the rattling yard.   Their wish was
  now ·

Under their fresh-elected chief to unwind

The mystery of the river to the main,

Glance at the virgin glories of its coasts,

Unfold to Europe their discovery,

And claim its government, as Cortez claimed

The rule of Mexico.—What thrill was theirs

Of still-succeeding ecstasy to trace

The panorama of the Amazons

Throughout the mighty river's thousand links,

Past selva and savanna to the sea !

What joy to feel their unimpeded bark

Leap in responsive rapture light along

As if, like some new creature come to life

Upon congenial element, it shared
The sanguine hopes, the mad impatient pulse
And keen delight of motion swift and free
That made them demigods, body and mind!
O, in those days and fairy-visioned nights,
Feeding on manna hopes that come no more
To this old worn-out earth, they lived indeed,
Breathing heroic air, and lifted high
Above the sordid cares that creep within
The guarded ease of villa nests, and make
The peasant's term a pitiable strife
With Hunger sniffing wolf-like at the door!

Forest and forest passed them, whirling west
With all their unclaimed grandeur : hill on hill
In the far distance, capped with snow-white
          quartz
Thin-veined with gold, rose up and sank adown,
Doing them stately homage : shady alleys
And sunlit glades in the dim columned woods
Opened and closed their beauties as they came :
Islets and infant archipelagos
Thronging their wavy pathway grew in size,

And shrank again behind them : rivers poured

Their roaring tribute from imperial urns

Into the main of waters where they rode

Almost invisible in midmost channel ;

For wide and wider grew the guarded banks,

As if the opening avenue must soon

With all its retinue of silent trees

End the long triumph of its thousand miles.

And here at last were towns and heathen fanes

Glittering with all the glory and the glow

Of occidental wealth ; and tawny chiefs,

Hung round with rubies and with emeralds,

Welcomed them from the shores ; and martial

    maids

Of Amazonian stature, breasted round

With plates of beaten gold, stood on the banks

And seemed to offer tribute, and entreat

The strangers' stay. Still on and on they sped

With all the glory of the Occident

Unrolling like a map before their eyes ;

Until, at last, their river voyage o'er,

They came one sunset within earshot of

The sullen roar of Ocean swinging ever
His billowy strength against the stolid land.
All night they listened to the measured beat
Booming along the dark: and at the dawn,
Lo, the far banks receding north and south
Never again to meet ! and the green sea
With all its millioned multitude of waves
Tumbling in chainless freedom ! and the sun
Slow-rising as of old with welcoming smile
Out of the depths of the familiar sea !

THE muffled boom of ocean far away
Is in mine ears again : but now no more
As in blue breakers whitening on the beach
Hear I the voice of cheerful energy,
Activity and change : it is the moan   `
Of baffled feebleness that flings in vain
A tangled waste of drenched and drownèd
      hopes
In final effort on the rocks of fate.

And sing ye may, ye mariners, who launch

Your gilded galleys in the freshening dawn
Upon a sunlit sea : to you the winds
Call joyous from the deep; to you the plain
Of ocean is a silver-fretten floor
Of sapphire luminous with the living gleams
Of the great crystal sky-dome over all.

And ye with faces brown that, homeward
    bound,
Press where the faded figurehead below
Looks towards the enlarging hills, and shout
    for joy
When on the far edge of the safe-crossed main
The old kirk-spire shoots up, the old round
    tower
At the pierhead, and on the concave shore
Houses and homes in social brotherhood
With open door waiting your late return
—Ye, too, may sing in heart, your labours o'er,
The quiet haven in your weary view,
And the calm lights of evening overhead
Steadily shining as the sun goes down.

But wonder not if on despondent lips
The voice of song has died, and querulous care
Breaking a silent grief draws nigh to them
Who on the ocean lost and far from home
Feel neither morning's flush of airy hopes
Nor evening's rest resigned—see neither sun
Nor lunar light nor stellar, wrapt in mist
And pelting rains that intermingle night
With dawnless day and unseen sea with land.

O dreary seas, your sullen leaden grey
Will ever sun enlace with gold again?
Will ever hope rise more in complete orb
Of brilliant song, Apollo with a crown
Of fresh-dug gold luting it o'er your sadness?

O many times in heedless ears shall sound
The solar melody, in heedless eyes
The solar blazon be outrolled above
Your leaden waters ! But to one to whom
These were the joy which youthful monarchs
        feel
When first they grasp a sceptre, nay, were life,

Were very life throbbing through all the veins
And arteries as with eternal pulse
—To Orellana, never, never more !

On him the shadow of the Hand of Death
Descended darkening, as a falcon's wing
Falls on the snowy radiance of a dove.
Oh, how should he escape that closing Hand?
Would the imperial parchment in his gripe,
With the vain sanction of its dangling seals,
Its signatures, its pomp of Latin phrase
That gave the wealth and width of the Brazils
From seashore to sierra westward far,
To Don Francisco Orellana, bribe?
Would prayer, or tear, or impious sacrifice
For just a little summer's lease of life
Such as an insect has, persuade ?   Would love
Of wife new-married by vicarious pain
Avert?
　　　　But what were all the wish of life,
Now hope of life was gone, for that one stain
Of perjury that blackened all the past?

The stain sent rays of gloom even to the
　realm
Of sunny infancy: and forward far
It rushed into Eternity, a flood
Of widening blackness! Orellana groaned
And hid his face with both his hands: "The
　star!"
He muttered in his agony—"The star!
Oh, I mistook it for the will of Heaven!"

Beside him where he tossed in fever-pain
In the dim narrow cabin sat his wife
With ne'er a word of comfort in her heart.
His men dotted the deck like images
Of famine and despair—hating both him
Who with a lying story lured them forth
To chase a madman's fancy, and themselves
Who credited a dreamer. Vainly they
Had thrust through mist and rain, through
　creek and strait
And muddy shallow, searching for a channel
To inland El Dorado:—in despair

Now waited for the end.   The rain-streams
    hissed
Along the deck, and all around the ship,
And on the sea, and all along the sea
To where the neighbour ships loomed through
    the mist
Like veilèd monuments; and at the window
Of the dim cabin where the leader lay
Hissed loudly; and in scornful hissings drowned,
Sank Orellana from the world of men.

B R I E R S

" There grows a *bonnie* brier buss in oor kailyard. "

—OLD SONG.

I.

IN MEMORIAM.

OUT there in the sunshine, that's gilding
The garden that seldom is green,
The workmen are lazily building
A pillar in praise of the Dean.

Last week they were at a church-steeple,
And next week it may be a jail:
—They're a common mechanical people,
You see, and their labour's for sale.

Two soldiers at them are gazing,
Schoolboys, and a loafer or two:

Asks one, "What is it they're raising?"
Another, "And what did he do?"

Pale Frank hurries past to the College,
Hollow-eyed, red-nosed, and lean ;
The way to get on is get knowledge,
And he's hoping one day to be Dean.

———*o*———

II.

THE MASK OF MISERY.

"'Thou art unto them as a very lovely song of one that hath
a pleasant voice and can play well on an instrument : for they
hear thy words but they do them not."

THE lattice is open, and into the street
Floats music sad and slow ;
To the midnight Bobby it's quite a treat
—Up there there's company, light, and heat,
And the luxury of woe.

Now none will say she cannot play,
  That lady at the keys ;
And the singer that beside her stands
With Gounod's music in his hands
  Can melt a soul with ease.

There is a green hill far away——
  And the passion sinks and swells.
—Do you think they believe it? that lady gay?
That silken tenor?   .   .   Or would you say
  It's a sound and nothing else?

Be this as it may, they dissipate
  The night with wailing psalms ;
And the rest of the company clap and prate,
While a waif from the Pleasaunce at the gate
  Sings merrily for alms.

III.

FOUND DEAD.

A LITTLE wayward human elf
  Lay dead at Cæsar's feet
Where sceptred Cæsar lifts himself
  Out of the vulgar street.

A passing workman at the dawn
  Of a December day,
He found this little doeless fawn,
  This " Home "-reared runaway.

A wild bud by the rude winds blown
  From its untended sod ;
A young life on the altar stone
  Flung to a pagan god.

They bore the slender fragile thing
  From Cæsar's feet of stone.
And who was she?—By their whispering
  A child of Cæsar's own.

IV.

THESE AND THOSE.

UNDER an apple-tree, laden
With pink promissory-notes,
Loiter a man and a maiden
—Each on the other one dotes.

Blue through the apple-boughs o'er them
It gleams like a sapphire, the sky ;
Rosy and radiant before them
Vistas invitingly lie.

Out of their sight and their hearing,
But only over the wall,
Two are snarling and sneering
Who love not each other at all.

What had you said had you seen them
As I have put them in rhyme ?
For these are those, and between them
Is only a measure of time.

H

V.

PARTING AND MEETING.

THEY quarrelled, parted with a frown,
　Took each his separate path,
And that and many a day went down
　And rose upon their wrath.

And Jim went east and Duncan west,
　And not a word said Jim ;
And Duncan—well, he would be blest
　Before he'd speak to him.

The tranquil hamlet of their birth
　The brothers left behind ;
Wider between them grew the Earth
　And keener blew the wind.　.　.　.

In 'Frisco where the cypress waves
　Its melancholy green,
Are James and Duncan Gordon's graves,
　And but a step between.

VI.

THE PLEADER.

It's an edifying sight to see
  His teeth like ivory shine
As he laughs with a lord familiarly
  Over the walnuts and wine :

Or as from court to court he skips,
  Too busy to look grand,
With a golden lie between his lips
  And truth half-choked in his hand.

Busy indeed !   And, little with big,
  And one time with another,
Must many a thought hive under his wig :
  —There's never one of his mother.

Over a tub in the village she bends,
  Red-armed amid the suds,
While he a titled rogue defends
  In town before my Luds.

VII.

DELILAH.

"Quod dicit amanti
In vento, et rapidâ scribere oportet aquâ."

SHE put an arm around his neck, and, looking
in his eyes,—
"For other love I nothing reck; 'tis yours alone
I prize."

She kissed his brow, she kissed his mouth, she
made his heart rejoice,—
"In all the land from north to south you are
my only choice."

—And yet he knew within a week, at most
within a year,
A like confession she might speak in some one
else's ear.

VIII.

THE TWO SUNSETS.

FINISHED, on the studio wall
   Hangs the painter's masterpiece ;
Round it crowd the critics all
   Gabbling like a flock of geese.

This is good, now !   That is splendid !
   —The foreshortening on that oak !
See how well the greys are blended !
   Ah ! but here's the master-stroke !

—So they gabble, heads awry,
   Craning all their necks together,
Just like geese when in the sky
   There's a change to dirty weather.

SAD at heart the painter pale
   Turns his back upon them all,
Watching down the long green vale
   Summer's sun in glory fall.

Pass unseen, translucent splendour !
   Change and pass, ye coloured fires !
Apes to art their homage render
   —Heaven's great pictures Art admires.

They will gabble over paint
   Till the night descending blind them,
Heedless of the gold that, faint,
   Fades, and fainter yet behind them.

IX.

THE PROMENADE.

HE beats his wife, who in the street
   Hangs smilingly upon his arm
With such a sad, pathetic, sweet,
And tremulous grace in the deceit
   —None but a devil could do her harm.

The crowds sail on, the coaches roll;
   And once, as former friends drove by,
One tearful glance at him she stole:
Yet this man with the little soul
   —He has a body six foot high.

X.

JOAN THAMSON'S MAN.

HE fears his wife, who in the street
 Leads him about from shop to shop;
His training is a thing complete,
He's taught to carry, and look neat,
 And stop wherever she may stop.

To-day I marked him when a shoal
 Of boisterous bachelors cantered by;
At them a greyhound glance he stole:
And this man of the little soul
 —His body's over six foot high.

XI.

WITHOUT AND WITHIN.

MARTIAL words to a mournful chant !
But martial words her patrons want
Where the bounce is big if the sense be scant
  —Though to her it's nothing at all ;
It happens to be some jingo rant
    Caught from a music-hall.

A white face hooded in a shawl,
Upon whose faded tartan fall
Prelusive hail-drops round and small
  In the blaze of the dram-shop seen :
—A tapster flings her a coin, and a call
    For " Jock o' Hazeldean."

Within, across a table bend

A drunkard and his drunken friend,

Who with the empty gill-stoup end

   Keeps time with noisy beat

To the song the girl he should defend,

   His wife, sings in the street.

XII.

THE AULD HOOSE AND THE NEW.

CLICK go the balls in the billiard-room,
   The glasses clink at the bar,
Mine host at the door looks into the gloom
   —Looks up at the evening star.

That star of old has looked too cold
   On a Cæsar's cinctured brow
To envy the gold whose links enfold
   The breast of a Boniface now!
And covet not, mine honest host,
   The treasury of heaven:
'Tis to enrich some beggar's ghost
   Yon gold will yet be given.

And here it comes adown the street.
   Slips into the window blaze
And sings with tremulous voice and sweet
   A song of eldern days.

The auld house, the auld house,
   What tho' the rooms were wee?
Kind hearts were dwellin' there
   And bairnies fu' o' glee!

The mavis still doth sweetly sing,
   The bluebell sweetly blaw,
The bonnie Earn's clear-windin' still—
   But the auld house is awa!

The Auld Hoose to the simple strain
   Rises in memory clear;
He sees the round-stone walls again,
   In youthful days so dear;
A bent old man with silver hair,
   His father! at the plough—
God! what avails the anguished prayer
   That he were living now?

He looks out into the vocal gloom,
   But his thoughts are wandering far,
While the balls go click in the billiard-room
   And the glasses clink at the bar.

FROM THE SICILIAN OF
VICORTAI

A DEDICATION.

LIKE spray blown lightly from the crested wave
      To glitter in the sun,
So from my heart love gave
      These airy fancies to the eyes of a
      belovèd one.
      But who shall guess
From the blown foam that in the sunbeam
      shines
      What secret stores there be
      Of unsunn'd sea?
      Ah! how much less
The depths of what I feel from these poor
      broken lines
      I dedicate to thee!

II.

REFLECTED HEAVEN.

THE mountain-tops above the mist
 Like summer islands lie—
Now we together both were blest
 If thither we could fly.
  And you, while at
  Your feet I sat,
Would gaze into the skies;
  But I would be
  Content to see
Their glory in your eyes.

III.

SUMMER IN WINTER.

Winter is it? Summer splendour
   Never was so fair to see !—
All because a maiden tender
   Gave to-day her heart to me.
Heaven a happy lifetime lend her,
   Long, and from all evil free ;
For the graces that commend her
   Make her life the life of me.

IV.

LOVE TEST.

LASSIE wi' the face sae bonnie,
    An' the bricht bewitchin' ee,
Is there, tell me, is there ony
    Danger I can dare for thee?
That I lo'e thee thou mayst know it,
    But it's hard for me to bear
A' my love till I can show it
    By some danger I maun dare!

V.

THE VIOLET'S GRAVE.

THE woodland ! And a golden wedge
  Of sunshine slipping through !
And there, beside a bit of hedge,
  A violet so blue !

So tender was its beauty, and
  So douce and sweet its air,
I stooped, and yet withheld my hand,—
  Would pluck, and yet would spare.

Now which were best?—for spring will pass
  And vernal beauty fly—
On maiden's breast or in the grass
  Where would you choose to die?

VI.

FELIX, FELIX TER QUATERQUE!

Shout and sing, ye merry voices
Of the mountain-forest free!
What, but late, were jarring noises
Now as music are to me!
Earth in bridal bloom rejoices,
Heaven benignly bends to see!
He, beloved of her his choice is,
Blest of all the boys is he!
Blest of all the world of boys is
He that's telling this to thee!
Shout and sing, ye merry voices!—
Fill the forest with your glee!

VII.

SUMMER EVE.

It is the hour when all things rest :
The sun sits in the bannered West
And looks along the golden street
That leads o'er ocean to his feet.

Sea-birds with summer on their wing
Down the wide West are journeying,
And one white star serenely high
Peeps through the purple of the sky.

O sky, and sea, and shore, and air,
How tranquil are ye now, and fair !
But twice the joy ye are were ye
If one that's dead companioned me.

VIII.

SERENADE.

AWAKE, beloved ! it is the hour
When earth is fairyland ;
The moon looks from her cloudy bower,
The sea sobs on the sand.
Our steps shall be by the dreaming sea
And our thoughts shall wander far
To the happy clime of a future time
In a new-created star !

Arise, my fair ! a strange new wind
Comes kindly down from heaven ;
Its fingers round my forehead bind
A chaplet angel-given.
I'll sing to thee of the dawns to be
And the buds that yet shall blow
In the happy clime of a future time
Which only the angels know !

IX.

THE FUGITIVES.

DEAR love, we have left them behind us !
  Behind us, and far below !
They will search a month ere they find us
  In the hill-wood where we go.

Listen ! . . . that is the voice of the forest,
  It is whispering us words of cheer :
Ah, my heart, when my heart was sorest,
  Has often been healed up here !

Why do you cling to me, darling,
  And bury your face in my breast ?
You may well be at ease where the starling
  Has grown a familiar guest.

The forest and the mountain
  And I are old, old friends,
And the wild birds and the fountain
  And the sky that over them bends;

And the friends of my youth and my childhood'
  Thou maiden of the sea
That hidest thy face in the wild wood,—
  How could they be foes to thee?

Look up, my own heart maiden!
  No foot of man comes here;
'Tis tenantless as Eden
  Throughout the tranquil year!—

But I am nearly forgetting
  Old Philip and his wife:
From sunrise to sunsetting
  They lead a simple life.

'Tis sixty years since he brought her
  To share his board and bed;

And they had a son and a daughter—
  But *she* is long since dead.

And the boy became a soldier
  And marched to the wars away :
And the old couple grow still older
  In the wood here where they stay.

How brightly your eyes are shining,
  And but the trace of a tear !
With your cheek on my arm reclining,
  Dear heart, you should have no fear.

They sit far up on the mountain
  Beside their clean-swept hearth,
Where the river is only a fountain
  And heaven is nearer than earth.

The goodwife knits her stocking,
  And Philip should trap the game ;
But he's old, so the birds are flocking
  And the blue hares are quite tame.

The mother thinks of her daughter
　And her hair that outshone the sun ;
But Philip dreams of slaughter,
　And of his wayward son.

There is none, you know, to advise her,
　Excepting her prejudiced mate.
Ah, heaven ! the mother is wiser
　As love is better than hate.

So the mother knits and fondles
　In fancy the flaxen hair,
While Philip a sabre handles,
　And starts in his sleep in his chair.

How far to their cottage is it ?—
　A good hour's climb, I should say :
Of course, we must pay them a visit,
　And they're sure to ask us to stay.

So now, sweetheart, if you're rested,
　We'll farther up the wood :

Many a night have I nested
  Here in the solitude.

It's grand in the wood in the sunlight
  As the sunlight's falling now,
But I like it too when the wan light
  Of the moon is on each bough.

Look back ! she is floating yonder—
  I saw her between the trees
When their fringes were drawn asunder
  By the fingers of the breeze.

How naked and forsaken
  She shrinks through the blue day-sky !
At night, never fear, she'll awaken
  And lift her horn on high.

Look up through the boles before us,
  And the long clear slanting lines
Where the light that shimmers o'er us
  Is sifted through the pines !

It's a good hour yet till gloaming,
 And then we've Selenë's light;
And it's pleasant this woodland roaming
 In search of a home for the night.

Give me your hand, my darling !
 We're safe in the solitude;
In the world beneath us there's snarling—
 There's peace in the mountain wood.

X.

THE DREAMER.

I ROAM a homeless spectre
Among the shows of Time,
For I have drunk the nectar
Of the eternal clime.
Oh, what is all the treasure
That Time or Earth bestows,
To one sip of the pleasure
My soul in dreamland knows?
With you in dreams I've wandered
The gates of Eden through,
And cheerfully have squandered
Life's morning hours for you.
Around me my relations
Came with their prayers and jeers :

I bore their scorn with patience,
I heard their love with tears.
Oh, what is all the treasure
That Time or Earth bestows,
To one sip of the pleasure
My soul in dreamland knows?
They tried to rouse with glory,
They sought to win with wine;
I smiled to hear their story
As they had smiled at mine.
To duties next they pointed
That I had left undone;
But I, love's pale anointed,
Would own to only one:
A duty that will lengthen
When theirs are past and o'er,
Eternity shall strengthen,
And I will value more.
There's one could tell how truly
My rital vows I've kept,
With what devotion duly
Both when I waked and slept.

In vain they promised glory,
In vain they proffered wine ;
I smiled to hear their story
As they had smiled at mine.
Their ease to me is aching,
They smile when I would weep,
Their sleep to me is waking,
Their waking only sleep.
Oh, what is all the treasure that Time or Earth
   bestows,
To one sip of the pleasure my soul in dream-
   land knows?

S Y L V Æ

K

THE GENIUS OF THE GLEN.

(A Ballad of the Sunless Summer.)

It was the glen so dear to us,
   And on the eve of May,
Yet ne'er a leaf was on the buss
   Or blossom on the spray.

The sky aboon was grey and still
   —Oh, something was to blame !
And immelodious flowed the rill
   That gives the glen its name.

Grey were the dripping craigs wi' fogg,
   The ferns were red and sere,
Dowie the day, as days that dog
   The wa-gaun o' the year.

And but ae gowan in a nook
　Had daured to ope its ee;
And, wae was I ! it seemed to look
　Reproachfully on me.

And mair than wae, amazed was I
　A flower o' gentle fame
Should lay its woodlan' shyness by
　And bid me bide a blame.

The linties on the scroggy brae,
　They hadna heart to sing;
In undertones they seemed to say
　"Ye've robbed us o' the spring!"

And wae and mair bewildered yet
　I waited for their sang :
Puir things ! I only heard them fret
　That winter days were lang.

The faded firs and larches tall
　On me looked darkly down,

They wagged their heads together all,
  And met me with a frown.

I turned me from the steep glen-side
  To glancing linn and pool :
The naiad down the water wide
  Fled with a sound of dule !

Oh, doubly dowie noo the glen,
  And drearer yet the sky,
And sad the winds that noo and then
  Complaining passed me by.

For I was mingled wi' the cause
  That wrought the season wrong,
Had somehow meddled wi' the laws
  That lead the months along ;

Had stolen the sunshine from the air,
  The greenery from the glen,
Had killed the querulous wren wi' care,
  And made the merle a wren.

O' whatna man could that be true?
—Surely he'd spare, I cried,
The glen in which he came to woo,
In which he won his bride.

I carved her name upon an oak
Last August, and since then
Although Glen Farg to ither folk,
To me 'tis Annet's glen.

And Scotland in its hundred nooks
Nae brawer glen can show,
Nor yet amang her hundred brooks
A burn sae dear I know.

And wae am I, and sad indeed,
Sae fair a glen should grieve
And wear the weary winter weed
Sae late as summer eve.

—Wi' that the day grew dim as e'en,
A glamour owre me fell,

And weird and foreign grew the scene,
    And far away as well.

And first a thin forwandered wind,
    As of a voice that grieves
Gaed up the glen, and left behind
    A rustling of red leaves.

And next a hush fell on the glen ;
    Nor move nor breathe could I ;
The hush sank into deeps, and then
    I heard a long-drawn sigh.

Then, from the shadow of a lirk
    That cleaves the grey glen wall
A reverend figure from the birk
    Rose like a tower, and tall.

His face was dusky red as leaves
    That burn with autumn fire :
Such tint the cedar-bough receives
    When summer suns retire.

Brown beechen leaves that once were green
  Composed his coat of mail,
And round his long white beard was seen
  A fringe of lichens pale.

And if the centuries had enlaced
  His cheek with many a line,
There was a vigorous freedom graced
  And made his look divine.

Upon his brow there sat awry
  A crown of faded fern,
And troubled was his coal-black eye,
  And grave his look, and stern !

And full on me he fixed his glance
  —Oh, but his glance was keen !
Like shimmer of a flying lance
  It dazzled baith my een !

" I am the Genius of the Glen,"
  He thus the silence brake,

"And thou——! Among the sons of men
  A falser never spake !

" Last August to this glen you brought
  A blithesome maid, and true ;
And when my fairest bower you sought,
  I welcomed both of you !

" I housed you in my fairest bower
  —True love is all so rare ;
It was a joy I feel this hour
  To see so kind a pair.

"And all my nymphs and naiads took
  A peep at where you lay,
Then hastening back to brake and brook,
  Talked of you all the day.

" So glad were they, so pleased was I ;
  And when you vowed to bring
The maiden with the sunbright eye
  This way again in spring,

" I vowed that spring might come or stay,
   But as for mine and me,
Our glen and we would not be gay
   Till she should come to see !

" And birds are mute, and flowers have slept,
   And trees delayed to leave ;
And sadly we our vows have kept
   Till summer's very eve.

" And here on summer's eve art thou,
   The falsest among men,
Who darest with a broken vow
   To enter Annet's glen ! "

His voice was stern, and anger blazed
   In baith his coal-black een :
"And this," he cried, with arm upraised,
   " Our welcome would have been ! "

A flash—a rush of opening leaves,
   A mist of emerald light,

And green with yellow interweaves
  A vision of delight !

A million myriad leaves and flowers,
  Where flowers and leaves were none ;
And where but late were sunless bowers,
  New gilded by the sun.

The sunshine on the soft green leaf
  Flowed down from broad blue skies :
—Oh me ! it was a dear relief
  To rest the weary eyes.

And merle and throstle sat or flew,
  And whistled loud and sang ;
And more and more their gladness grew,
  Till all the valley rang.

And down the glen the water ran,
  With pleasure plashing cool ;
And roses blushed, and lilies wan
  Grew pale by every pool.

The flaunting woodbine o'er the rocks
    Held out its honeyed horn ;
The belted bees flew past in flocks
    And incensed with the morn.

The broom was fringed with golden flame,
    And through the woodland wide
A wind that wandered without aim
    Grew sad for joy, and sighed.

Dear Lord ! it was a pleasant sight
    To see but in a dream—
The green leaves, and the holy light,
    And the clear, flowing stream.

Sure Eden glimpses yet are got,
    And Eden memories ours,
While summer's golden glance is shot
    Through woodbine-birken bowers !

But now the whole air seemed to dance,
    The glen went whirling round,

And falling in a slumbrous trance
  I lay along the ground.

How long in this deep sleep I lay
  I have not to declare,
But when I woke the sky was grey,
  The birks and larches bare ;

The maniac wind, that takes no care
  Whether 'tis glad or grieves,
Was scattering in the beamless air
  Handfuls of autumn leaves.

30th April 1879.

THE MEET AT MIDNIGHT.

31ST DECEMBER 1878.

THEY are mustering to-night on the ocean
  Their legions in mighty force,
Their banners in wild commotion,
  Their trumpets braying hoarse.

The billows are scourged into madness
  By the stroke of their giant wings,
And the hollow vault that holds the stars
  Booms, and bellows, and rings !

Would you know why all this gathering
  Of winds at the midnight hour?
—I will tell you anon, but you must know
  First of their mighty power.

They have come from the south, and the east-
  ward,
And the fierce north blasts are there ;
And shoulder to shoulder with rumpled wings,
  They press till they fill the air !

For miles and for miles of the ocean,
  Shoulder to shoulder they lie,
And the long strong sweep of their flanking
  wings
  Strikes from sea to sky.

You might trace the track they have come by
  By lighthouses down thrown,
And towns with steeples and churches
  And the sea with wrecks o'erstrewn.

And their squadroned strength is greater
  Than ever yet shook the earth,
When she shakes with the mighty anguish
  Of an earthquake at the birth.

But now they are all in motion,
And with one continuous shout
They sweep in a hurricane up Strathbraan,
And blow the Old Year out !

For the burden of sin on the Old Year's back
As he sways and staggers along,
Is as big as the huge earth-globe itself,
And needs a wind so strong.

Blow, winds from the German Ocean,
This burden from the earth !—
Sweet rest be yours and the weary world's
In the hush of the Young Year's birth !

SIMMER LOST:

A SIGH FOR SANDIE IN NEW ZEALAND.

Hoo sweet were simmer i' the woods,
    Or doon the burnie clear,
—In a' her haunts, in a' her moods,—
    If, Sandie, you were here.

Then doobly graun the wastlin braes
    Wad glow at gloamin-tide,
An' redder wad the mornin' rays
    Rin up the plantin-side.

An' bonnier owre the loch wad creep
    The dimplin' waves sae sma',
An' wins less wantonlie wad sweep
    The young green leaves awa'.

L

And I should look wi' clearer een
Aboot me an' before,
An' cease to think o' simmers, been
To be again no more.

It's simmer yet, an' yet a'most
I mourn the simmer gane,
An' feel as if its joys were lost
Lavisht on me mylane.

A GIFT FOR A BRIDE.

A GIFT for my bride on her birthday!
—But what shall the souvenir be?
What best of all gifts of the earth may
      Remind her of me?

A ring for her delicate finger,
  To pinch it a little all day?
A song in her heart that will linger
      When I am away?

A chain for her neck, with a locket?
  A book that her mind will engage,
And will easily go in her pocket?
      A bird in a cage?

A volume of manuscript verses?
  A flower in porcelain that blows?
A phial of scent that disperses
              The attar of rose?

The frond of a fern, or a feather,
  Among her fair tresses to twine?
A sprig, for her breast, of white heather,
              Or pale jessamine?

A thimble? a bangle? a bonnet?
  A pencil? a portrait of me?
A bracelet with *AEI* upon it?
              A crooked bawbee?

Now which of them all shall I send her?
  Indeed I might send her them all,
" *With care*," "*Carriage paid*," "*Special tender*,"
              —And think it too small.

Suppose I just send her a letter
  And sign it in silver " YOUR OWN " ?
—Bah ! either I'll manage it better,
          Or leave it alone !

That notion is too mediocre :
  —Come, Fancy ! there's something amiss !
—I have it ! As I am a smoker,
          I'll send her a kiss !

But how to transmit it ! . . . What fairy,
  Or seraph, or sylph of the air
Will come in my present quandary
          My offering to bear?

I'll cleanse my mustache of tobacco,
  And wait for a wind from the south
To take the dear trifle, *per Bacco!*
          Direct from my mouth.

Receive it, ye breezes ! And lest ye
  Should lose it, or make a misdeal,
Take ten or twelve more to attest the
        Devotion I feel !

Your flight is up over yon mountain
  That looks o'er Strathearn to Strathtay,
Then down by the clear caller fountain ;
        —At Craigie you stay.

And there, to the mirthfullest lady
  That ever was sad in the sun,
Deliver your trust ; but be ready
        To go when it's done !

—And how will ye know when ye've found
      her ?
  —Her gait, and the grace of her glance,
The beauty that brightens around her,
        Will tell you at once !

She's true, and she's kind, and she's clever,

And pensive, and not very tall

—As high as my heart is, however—

And modest withal.

And so, unannounced, you'll enfold her;

And, ere from your wings she can slip,

You'll softly pay down, while you hold her,

My tax on her lip.

THE CAMP ON THE OCHILS.

"Et propinquâ luce fulsere signa: . . . et Romanis redit animus: . . . et fuit atrox in ipsis portarum angustiis proelium, donec pulsi hostes."—TACITI *Agricola*, xxvi.

THE gold has paled to silver on the height,
   The gull belated to the lake has flown ;
Why sits young Andro in the house to-night
   While Cæsar hunts in the old camp alone ?

The goodman's cutting clover in the field,
   Young Phemie o'er the meadow calls the cow :
They've all a task but Cæsar—idle chield !
   Cæsar stands whining on the whinny knowe.

How would his ears go up, his eyes grow clear,
   The white star on his tail be whisked about,

If only Andro's bonnet should appear
  Above the dike, followed by Andro's shout !

What fun you'd see in the old camp ! What
    bounds
  O'er burrowy mound and boulder, furze and
    heath !
Andro would beat — Cæsar would watch the
    grounds,
  His pink tongue palpitating o'er his teeth !

Where lingers Andro ?—Harvesting the light
  For one red page beside the kitchen flame :
A different Roman is the spell to-night,
  And Tacitus, not Cæsar, is the name !

The page is open where Agricola's camp
  One daybreak, eighteen centuries ago,
Sprang to a man from earth-bed cold and damp
  At the wild slogan of the Celtic foe.

The battle's in the gateways, hand to hand;
  The sword of Caius rings on Colin's mace;
The eagles flash—who can their glance with-
    stand?
    On them! They yield—the rout becomes a
    race!

How strange it seems,—the ruined camp with-
    out,
  With peaceful rabbits hopping to and fro;
Within, the schoolboy glorying in the rout
  Of his forefathers there so long ago!

ADVENTUS VERIS.

SPRING came to-day! and glad were we
As very children in our glee.
The sun shone forth with blinding flame,
And from the west a soft wind came:
The west! Nay, sister, rather say
It blew from boyhood's happy day!
It brought with it the village old
Wherein was passed our age of gold,
And I, a happy-hearted scholar
With jacket short and broad white collar,
Frisked with my classmates in the street:
—Ay me! how fast the seasons fleet!

Spring came to-day! Our minstrel, mute
No longer, tuned and tried his flute;

Puss in the window-corner heard,
Looked cageward, closed her eyes, and purred;
And outside in the open air
Sparrows shot whirring here and there;
And one old ragged meagre rook
Who, feeling beauish, rashly took
A sunward voyage, venturing high
Was buffeted about the sky.

Spring came to-day: she called us out
With a right cheery country shout.
We spied her through the blackthorn hedge,
We saw her in the lakeside sedge,
We traced her footsteps o'er the hill,
We chased her down the rippling rill,
We lost her in a miry lane,
But in Craiglockhart copse again
We sought the merry gipsy, chiding,
And caught her in a hollow hiding.

Spring came to-day: the hawthorn buds,
The crystal of the Pentland floods,

The sword-like sedges by the lake,
The red-tipt branches in the brake,
The thin clean braird of new-year's grass,
Gowans that open as you pass
—Their wide-awake fresh fearless eyes
Glowering surprised at *your* surprise—
And balmy airs, and skies of blue
Convince you that the news is true.

We tarried as the sun went down
On yon high hill besouth the town,
But fairest view, of all we spied,
The gardened homes of Morningside.
The ploughman half a field away
Rested his horses on the brae,
Leaned o'er his plough, and on the air
Came pattle-raspings of the share ;
Then overglanced the furrows drawn
By his stout greys and him since dawn,
Took snuff, clicked with his cheek and tongue,
Shook the plough-line and *snooved* along !

How sweet it was to see a star
Born in the heavenly blue afar !
To mark the slowly waning light,
The coy approach of veilèd Night ;
To see domestic lights appear
In villa windows far and near ;
And hear upon our homeward way
The children singing at their play,
Their fresh young voices rising sweet
Out of the dim suburban street!

Spring came to-day : let's dedicate
The evening hours to celebrate
Her joyous advent, sister mine !
—And first, a glass of generous wine ;
Then fruit ; and strew the room with flowers
To dull the footfall of the hours ;
And you will sing when I am mute,
And I will choose a tale to suit
The sweet occasion—*What You Will*
Or *As You Like It :* Shakespeare still

For every season has a say
   A mood for every man ;
And so we'll mark SPRING CAME TO-DAY
   As well as ever we can !

———o———

THE LAD OF BENARTY.

Happy the man wha belangs to nae party,
But sits in his ain hoose an' looks at Benarty.

ON the dome of the Lomond I lie
   With my head on a bed of red heather ;
I see but the clouds and the sky,
   But whether above me, or whether
Below me, I care not a fly
          Or a feather !

Far down in the town there's a din
　Where the blues are abused by the yellows,
For the yellows are likely to win
　And the blues are resentful and jealous;
—I laugh in my sleeve and my skin
　　　　　At the fellows !

And happy the chappie, say I,
　Who sails in the tail of no party:
He laughs as he looks to the sky
　With a laugh that is low down and hearty;
Or he sits in his house with his eye
　　　　　On Benarty!

PINES AND BOULDER.

"The whole creation groaneth and travaileth in pain."

THESE gloomy pines upon the heath,
 That in the sunlight sigh—
Their secret they will not bequeath,
 Nor will it with them die.

The cold stone they moan around
 Crusted with lichen grey—
It will not waken from its swound
 Till peals the Judgment-day !

A horror of the midnight dark
 Sleeps in that slumbering stone !
A shower of blood-drops on their bark
 Has made these pine-trees moan !

M

THE TWO FLOWERS.

" Learn by a mortal longing to ascend
Towards a higher love."

THERE's a cleft high up on the bare hillside
    That looks like a fairy bower ;
The prospect is fair and far and wide,
    And the fairy is a flower.
—Why do you nod, little one, up there
    At your watch-tower window so high ?—
I like to feel the caressing air,
    And I love to be near the sky!

There's a mossy cell in a sunken vale
    In the depths of a forest dim
Where a tiny flower is hiding pale,
    Her eyes with tears o'erswim.
—Why do you shrink, little one, down there
    In your sunless nunnerie ?—
I fear he will kiss me, the wandering air,
    And the big sky frightens me !

IN THE KNOCK-WOOD.

COME up and hear the pine-trees sigh!
Come up within their shade, and lie
And let the peace which they impart
Sink soothingly within your heart.

The sigh they send from every leaf
Breathes resignation and relief;
If there's a sadness in the tone,
You put it there yourself alone!

Each in its own allotted place
Lifts as it were to Heaven its face,
The while it stretches out the hand
Of friendship to the forest band.

Here are no jarrings and no jeers,
No fevered haste, no vexing fears,
No envious wish that will not wait,
No jealous blasphemy of Fate.

There's pathos in the patient air
With which their annual wrong they bear,
—Forgetful of the winter's blast
And glad the summer's come at last.

A placid pensiveness pervades
The mighty mountain-forest shades,
—A pensiveness that has no fear,
No shame, of past or future year.

Come, plunge you in their solitude ;
The bath will prove a double good
—A Styx for strength, for sinful pain
A Lethe to the sleepless brain.

THE LIGHT ON THE HILLSIDE.

" You see it gleaming far up the height,
Yon little square patch of warm red light?
—It's a far way up, but it's full in my sight,
And I lodge within its warmth to-night.

Around it the mists of the mountain are curled,
Above it the Night like a flag is unfurled,
But it shines like Milton's pendent World
With the bluster of Chaos against it hurled !

It's only a simple shepherd's cot ;
But there isn't in all the earth a spot
Where half so hearty a welcome is got,
—And *that's* the charm of home, is it not?

Within, my father is dozing through tire,
My mother is plying the twinkling wire,
Between them stands in front of the fire
A chair that encloses my heart's desire.

Its back ascends an enormous height,
Its arms stretch outward to left and right,
And it's clothed from top to bottom quite
In a clean chintz wrapper of blue and white.

But many wet bushes the winds will toss
Against my cheek; and one long moss,
And braes and brooks, I must climb and cross,
Ere I cover the miles between it and Kinross.

—Good night, fellow-student! Good night,
    good night!
A couple of hours will see me all right :
Think of me then in my chair on the height,
Think of me then—and you'll envy me quite !"

How strangely his voice at parting thrilled !
—Well, the night wore by, and the storm was
    stilled,
And morning dawned ; but the Fates had
    willed
That chair on the mountain should never be
    filled !

——*o*——

HEIGH-HO ! THE WIND AND
THE RAIN !

DAY had come without dawning,
    The street was deserted and still,
At the mill-door the miller stood yawning
    With his back to the hum of the mill.

We drove past the mill with a clatter,
    And out on the wind-swept plain,
And then down came, whole water,
    In gleaming sheets the rain.

The road struck up the mountains
　Suddenly ere we wist,
We heard the gushing of fountains
　And the wail of mews in the mist.

At times through the grey fog stealing
　Swept columns of ghostly pines,
Behind us they seemed to be wheeling
　And forming in squares and lines.

And once far up at a turning
　Where a loch feeds a hundred rills,
We were ushered without warning
　Into a conclave of hills.

Like hooded monks before us
　They loomed through mist and rain :
The swirling mists closed o'er us
　And they were lost again.

Splish ! splash ! on the flat of the mountain
　Stumbles our jaded beast ;

The jolts are past all counting,
  And the rain has never ceased !

For dull monotonous mileage
  The hills in a mist have the palm
—I wish I were back in the village,
  Or sound asleep where I am.

———o———

Yᴇ FATE OF Yᴇ BOOK.

I WROTE a book ; and, what was worse,
I wrote the whole of it in verse.

Then upspoke an evil elf
—" Be a credit to yourself ! "
So I printed it, and sent it forth
West, and east, and south, and north.

Just as it left my hand I woke,
And the elfin spell that bound me broke ;

And I wished as I saw it o'erfly the land
That I had it back again in my hand ;
But the elf laughed loud with malicious glee
—" It may not be, and it may not be !
The cage is empty, the bird is free ! "—
And his mocking came back on the winds to
    me.

Then came forth the critic men
With sharp nose and sharper pen ;
They flung their long fingers into the sky
And caught the book as it fluttered by ;
And it shook like the wings of a captured bird,
And then, like a dead thing, hung ; nor stirred
As they bore it off with a strange dark smile.
But *my* heart was beating fast all the while.

From the free fresh air to a sunless gloom
They hurried it into a secret room :
The door swung back with a boding boom,
" And here," they said, " we will write your
    doom."

They pierced and probed it with their pens,
Examined it with a powerful lens,
And up and down they viewed and reviewed,
Till the good was bad and the bad was good,
Till white was black, and B was A ;
—But they used my book in a frightful way;
For its wings they broke and its back they
    bent,
And rumpled its feathers to their hearts' con-
    tent.

They then sat down at two long tables,
Dipt into ink, and wrote out labels ;
The while, most piteous to be seen,
My book lay ruined and wrecked between,
And meekly bore the dissecting glances
That stung my heart like a shower of lances.

At last one rose at the right-hand table
And read aloud from the written label—
" Though he may not have an eagle's pinion,
Yet the upper air is his dominion."

"And so say I, and I've written it so,"
Said Number Two; "he has wings of snow;
My judgment is that a swan is he."

"A swan!" from the left hissed Number Three,
"A swan!—I've a different tale to tell:
He's a gosling; I know the bird right well!"

Said a Fourth, with a head like a downy owl,
" It's a very ordinary barn-door fowl:
A useful creature, no doubt, in its place;
But a cackler! DIXI—that is, it's the case!"

" I agree so far with Number Four,"
Said Number Five, "as the barn-door:
But I made an inspection nice and narrow
And I pledge my ears the bird's a sparrow!
—And where's the critic will gainsay
That pledge of mine goes a good long way?"

Out to the centre stalked Number Six:
" Your various verdicts I must mix;

He's a bird has caught the various tone
Of other birds, but has none of his own.
It's a great pity, too, for he imitates well;
But all that he has he got outside his shell
—You know what I mean—he belongs to the
    breed
That pick up their song as they pick up their
    seed.
—I may add in your ear, but don't let it be
    known,
He has plagiarised from a bird of my own !"

" Yah! yah!" they all yelled, " it's a very good
    lark
That bird of your own : you were best keep it
    dark !"

Uprose Number Seven.   He, staggering, rose;
And I will not do more than refer to his nose :
" My masters "—he spoke rather thick—" are
    you blind ?
I've examined him—*hic!*—and what do I find ?

—He has wings that will soar with the best
  we have had;
But I hate him for all : at his best he is bad !"

Upspoke Number Eight, while he tore what he
  wrote,—
" I think him a bird of original note,
But I cannot be sure; so let's damn him as
  dunce;
He ought to come out more decided at once.
If he isn't a dunce I'm a Dutchman? So be
  it !
If he is—you will own I'm sagacious to see it !"

Scarce two agreed, till they fell on a plan
Which seemed to please them every man—
At least the hubbub ceased : they took
And hung their verdicts round my book
Like flags of all nations on a wreck,
Or labels on a phial's neck
Which each describes the draught to be
Sherry, laudanum, cold beef-tea.

They dragged it then to the door of their den
And gave it to the air again.

And away like a guilty thing it flew,
That thinks it a crime to live, to you;
And you took off the labels and stroked its
    wing,
And my poor book looked like another thing.
And now it was plain they all had erred
In naming it that and the other bird,
For it grew in the keep of those I love
A homely plain domestic dove.

THE FIFTEENTH OF AUGUST.

Now, while above heaven's windows dim and
    darken,
  And shadows shoot and grow,
And the wild peaks of rocky Thelemarken
  Blacken the evening glow,—

My thoughts come back from roaming o'er far
    places,
  Like sea-birds to their isle ;
And here in Norway bonnie Scottish faces
  Look through the gloom, and smile.

I know them all: it is a birthday meeting,
  And she, the birthday Queen,
Looks round as she receives each kindly greet-
    ing
  For one, who is not seen.

There's mirth, and music, and the chink of
glasses,
Laughter, and lights, and flowers;
—And so they pelt with roses, as he passes,
Time, and his train of hours.

The lights are out at last, the guests departed,
Yet, lingering near the gate,
There's one, I know, is listening gentle-hearted,
Although the night be late.

She feels almost a lover's kind caresses,
Hears his approaching feet:
—'Tis but the night wind in her wavy tresses,
Or blowing down the street.

Retire, sweet lass! in vain you look and hearken
For steps that are not near;
His path is through the wilds of Thelemarken,
Whose voice you think you hear.

N

The vision fades — fade all the much-loved
  faces,
  Fade Perth, Kinnoull, and Tay;
And unfamiliar outlines fill their places
  And gloom athwart my way.

I hear but in the wood the torrent calling
  In tones that come and go,
I feel but from the fells a silence falling
  Into the vand below.

And now above heaven's windows fairly
  darken,
  And earth is black and drear:
—And what do I afar in Thelemarken
  From all my heart holds dear?

WORKING AND IDLING.

WHILE some attempt the task on stirks,
  And some on mules or asses,
The man, that best could do it, shirks
  The gallop up Parnassus.

His Pegasus unsaddled feeds
  Beside him in a hollow,
Close by the rocky path that leads
  Up to thy heights, Apollo!

And idling in the shade he lurks,
  While they tug at their bridles;
They well may call their efforts WORKS;
  And what are his but IDYLS?

BLOOMTIME : A SONG.

My life is in its bloomtime,
  And faded sisters say—
" We've all our summer sometime,
  She need not look so gay."

But oh ! the wild young fellows,
  They compliment one so !
And then, to have *them* jealous
  —It's more than praise, you know !

A DITHYRAMB.

I.

LIFT up your voices in fraternal chorus,
All ye who share
The joyous spirit of the poet,
Wheresoe'er
In the four corners of the earth ye dwell!
—Lift up your voices!   Tell
Its owners earth is fair!
Sing!   Shout aloud, and show it!
Sing! for the earth is fair!
The same blue heaven is bending o'er us,
The same green earth extends before us,
And heaven is kind and earth is fair
—But mankind do not know it!
Lift up your voices

Till the world rejoices
And knows that earth is fair !

II.

What though we stand in sundered lands
And sing in several voices?
The brotherhood has many bands,
But with one heart rejoices.

III.

From the same Father-God we came,
To the same Father-God we go ;
Our hopes above are all the same,
—The same our griefs below,
Our sadness !

IV.

Sing ! till the night of sorrow
Is frightened from the land !
Give into every hand
The torch of gladness !

—Gladness is a flame
Increasing if you lend or if you borrow—
And cry aloud ! proclaim
At midnight everywhere
Good morrow ! and *good morrow !*
Till timorous souls leap from their hidings
And know that earth is fair !—
Lift up your voices
Till the world rejoices !
Sing ! till the surging air
Beats on the battlements of heaven the tidings
That man rejoices for the earth is fair !

COMPOSING A SONNET.

I.

COMPOSING a sonnet
'S like kindling a fire :
Heap largely upon it
—The spark will expire !

II.

Your very best "chance" is
To coax it with rhyme,
Then try it with fancies
—A touch at a time.

III.

Now lay the lines lightly,
Keep blowing between,
And soon it will brightly
Seize all the fourteen !

DAVID.

HE sits above the mists of Time,
 Above the poet throng;
He sits on morning heights sublime
 The king of choral song.

All lesser bards on lower heights
 Fall at his feet their lyres,
Unknown to them his high delights
 —Unfelt his far desires!

They sing of mortal grief and mirth
 In measures sweet to hear:
His song ambitious spurning earth
 Makes for Jehovah's ear!

He soars unmated and alone
Into eternal day,
The angel-host around the throne
Clear for his wing a way !

The Sons of Morning left behind
Cease after him to sing,
Not theirs that fervour of the mind
That fury of the wing !

The burning offering of his praise
To heaven himself bears he,
And with impetuous ardour lays
Even on Jehovah's knee !

No seraph's fear his soul can tame,
Nor cherub overawed ;
To him with first and foremost claim
Jehovah is a God !

The universe through all its bounds
　Is but a means of praise,
An orchestra of many sounds
　Concerting with his lays !

Hark, how to his conducting rod
　He calls creation's train
To hymn the praises of *his* God,
　And swell *his* choral strain !

PSALM CXLVIII.

PRAISE we the Lord ! Begin, ye matchless
　　creatures,
　The first-born of His might,
Circling His glory till your young-God features
　Absorb the eternal Light !
Take up the song, ye Seraphim ! Prolong,
　Ye Cherubim, the pæan !
Drown with His praise, ye meaner angel-
　　throng,
　The echoing Empyrean !

Praise Him, thou vast of space, that, like an
    ocean,
  The eternal heavens between
And the mysterious maze of starry motion,
  Stretchest afar serene !
Praise Him, ye Powers, that occupy with
    light
  Creation's outer porches,
Fronting the chaos of primeval Night
  With the eternal torches !

Praise Him, thou Sun, that from the flames of
    Morning
  Upleapest crowned with light !
Praise Him, thou Moon, retiring and returning
  To shepherdess the night !
Praise Him, ye wanderers of the Milky
    Way!
  Ye whispering Constellations !
Ye Comets ! and ye Meteor Stars that stray
  To unknown destinations !

Awake, thou Earth ! and wake thy slumbering
    legions,
  And shout aloud, and show
The challenge of the Everlasting Regions
  Is answered from below !
Praise Him, ye Winds, that sweep the deep
    sublime !
  Ye lower Seas and Surges !
Praise Him, ye Thunders of the torrid clime !
  Praise Him, ye Polar Scourges !

Praise Him, ye Clouds, ye stately sailing Foun-
    tains !
  Ye Cataracts and ye Rills !
Ye floating Icebergs and ye burning Moun-
    tains !
  Ye Deserts and ye Hills !
Praise Him, ye Earthquakes, from your secret
    mines !
  Ye rushing Avalanches !
Praise Him, ye congregated Palms, ye Pines !
  —Forests with all your branches !

Praise Him, ye Camels and ye Flocks domestic,
  That whiten the green plain !
Praise Him, thou Terror of the Woods, majestic
  With turbulence of mane !
Praise Him, ye Herds upon a thousand
  hills !
Ye Colts, without a rider,
That drink the freedom of the desert rills,
  Praise Him, the All-provider !

Praise Him, thou Eagle, from thy pinions fling-
  ing
  A twilight o'er the sea !
Praise Him, ye Doves !   Praise Him, ye Swal-
  lows, winging
  O'er isles and oceans free !
Praise Him, ye Sons of Eve, of all estates,
  Kindreds, and tongues, and nations !
Praise Him, ye Kings, ye sceptred Potentates !
  Ye Priests, with heart oblations !

Praise Him on chord, and reed, and with your
    voices,

  All peoples, maids, and men !

Praise Him together, while the heaven rejoices

  Answering the earth again !

Praise *Him* alone, for He alone is great

  Beyond all mark and measure ;

And we are but His handiwork, who wait

  Well pleased upon His pleasure !

OUR MARY: HER FATE.

This was Mary twenty years ago—
　　Mary then was four from twenty,
　　Mary then was gimp and genty,
　　Mary then had beaux a-plenty,
　　　Rosy cheeks and brow of snow;
　　　　Like a fairy
　　　　Was our Mary
　　　Twenty years ago.

This was Mary nineteen years ago—
　　Mary then was meek and modest,
　　Neatly ankled, shapely bodiced,
　　By the village poets goddessed,

Classed with Dame Demeter's Oe ;
　　Like an airy
　　Sylph was Mary
Nineteen years ago.

This was Mary eighteen years ago—
　　Mary properly deported,
　　Chastely with her sisters sported,
　　Would not kiss though she was courted,
　　　Coaxed by many a downy beau ;
　　　Wise and wary
　　　Was our Mary
　　Eighteen years ago.

This was Mary seventeen years ago—
　　When the lads their longing uttered
　　Nothing in her bosom fluttered,
　　And she neither stayed nor stuttered
　　　When she simply said them *No !*
　　　—Feeling *nary*
　　　Had our Mary
　　Seventeen years ago !

o

This was Mary sixteen years ago—

 When the men their custom carried

 Off to other marts, and married,

 Though it tested those that tarried,

  Mary her *ain gate* would go ;

   Veer nor vary

   Would our Mary

  Sixteen years ago.

This was Mary fifteen years ago—

 It was at a Christmas party

 That the spinsters at *écarté*

 Leapt up, startled by a hearty

  Smack beneath the mistletoe ;

   " Did he ?—dare he ? "

   " *Yes !* " said Mary

  Fifteen years ago !

RETURN TO EDINBURGH AFTER THE HOLIDAYS.

An' noo, fareweel to hills an' braes,
    To wuds an' watters broon !
We've pairtit wi' the holidays
    —They're aff ! they're fairly flewn !
An' we, wi' torn an' suddled claes,
    An' tired fra cuit to croon,
Wi' scartit hauns an' blistered taes,
    Are hirplin' back to toon !

Like laddies, ill for an excuse
    For havin' played *the tru'n*,
We're comin' in a kind o' daze,
    An' dummies every loon !
The ne'er a lauch hae we to raise
    To hud oor hearts aboon ;
—E'enoo we'd raither dee nor praise
    Oor ain pedantic Toon !

THE WEETS O' BAIGLIE.

HERE in the dinsome city pent
I think upon the days I spent,
The peacefu' days o' deep content
  Up on the Weets o' Baiglie.

It wasna that the sun shone through
Sky-deeps o' saft divinest blue,
It wasna for the famous view
  Up on the Weets o' Baiglie.

It wasna that the hills were green,
The wuns an' waters clear an' clean
—Baith bath an' balm to lungs and een
  Up on the Weets o' Baiglie.

It wasna that the fare was guid,
A hamely healthfu' change o' fuid,
A benefit to brain an' bluid,
    Up on the Weets o' Baiglie.

—An' there was ham, an' hare, an' veal,
Paitricks an' parritch, milk an' kail,
An' buttered scones o' barley-meal
    Up on the Weets o' Baiglie.

An' links o' puddins, black to see,
An' yowe-milk kebbuck, sweet to pree,
An' bickerfu's o' barley-bree
    Up on the Weets o' Baiglie.

It wasna that the folk were kind,
Baith laird an' tenant, herd an' hind,
An' no' a cratur ill-designed
    Up on the Weets o' Baiglie.

—The lasses bonnie, blithe, an' clean,
Douce i' the mornin, daft at e'en,
An' saxty soupple as saxteen
      Up on the Weets o' Baiglie.

The grannie's een as gleg as fowre,
The hauflin wi' his stirk-like glowre,
The fairmer lauchin' oot a' owre
      Up on the Weets o' Baiglie.

It wasna for the social noise
O' stack-yaird jinks an' fireside joys
An' rantin' wanton plays an' ploys
      Up on the Weets o' Baiglie.

It wasna for the hairvest wark,
The music o' the mornin' lark,
An' *leadin'* till the gloamin' dark
      Up on the Weets o' Baiglie.

It wasna juist the want o' care,

The change o' jacket, change o' air,

An' wastlin' wuns amang your hair

      Up on the Weets o' Baiglie.

It wasna ane—it was them a'

Upgaithered in a kind o' ba'

That gars me noo the days reca'

      Up on the Weets o' Baiglie.

Toon's bairns an' bodies! I could greet

To think you sin, an' never see't

—A Paradise itsel' complete

      Up on the Weets o' Baiglie.

Oh, gie the student his degree,

The advocat' his hansel fee,

But keep the joys that are for me

      Up on the Weets o' Baiglie!

Come roon' again, ye simmer suns!
An' burn wi' fragrant flame the whuns
That nod sae sweetly to the wuns
          Up on the Weets o' Baiglie.

An' set me on the hilly road
That leads to Uncle Rab's abode,
And I will praise the Lord my God
          Up on the Heights o' Baiglie.

SONNETS

APRIL.

Yonder comes April, on her lip a smile
   And in her eye a tear ! She has the look
   Of one whose face is as an open book
Yet thinks her harmless secret safe the while.
Her half-aversion is a childish wile
   To win a welcome from you ; in the nook
   Of the sweet eye a tear has just forsook
Lurks a blue ring that would a saint beguile !
—How shall we welcome her? Why, as a
      child
   Returning from a ramble, half afraid
Her absence may have vexed her mother mild,
   While through the pathless woods alone she
      strayed ;
And waiting till her father once has smiled
   And spread his arms and called his little
      maid.

NIGHT.

NIGHT lifts her shadowy arms above the earth,
  And breathes a benediction o'er the town;
  And eyes are closed, and aching heads go
    down,
And silence sits by the forsaken hearth.
And now in dreams to pale neglected Worth
  Come recognition and a cool green crown,
  And these have friends for every waking
    frown
And those for every misery now have mirth.
O blessèd sleep! that like a curtain nightly
  Drops on this tragi-comedy of man.
And blessèd, too, ye heaven-sent dreams, that
    rightly
Transform the piece to the original plan.
But best the buskined close—however lightly
  Hope slipped the sock on when the play began!

A BACK-LYING FARM.*

I.

[A back-lying farm but lately taken in;

  Forlorn hill-slopes and grey, without a tree ;

  And at their base a waste of stony lea

Through which there creeps, too small to make

    a din,

Even where it slides over a rocky linn,

  A stream, unvisited of bird or bee,

  Its flowerless banks a bare sad sight to see.

All round, with ceaseless plaint, though spent

    and thin,

  Like a lost child far-wandered from its home,

  A querulous wind all day doth coldly roam.

Yet here, with sweet calm face, tending a cow,

  Upon a rock a girl bareheaded sat

Singing unheard, while with unlifted brow

  She twined the long wan grasses in her hat.]

* The first part of this sonnet, which has already appeared
in the author's earlier volume of poems, is here reproduced as
an introduction to its second part.

II.

So sat the maiden : to the outward eye

  The flower-like genius of a flowerless waste,

  Dropped from the hand of Providence in haste

And left neglected here to wane and die.

—And yet, who knows what youthful fancies,

    ay,

  What heavenly visitants descending graced

  That lonely life, and with bright dreams dis-

    placed

The cloudy terrors of the natural sky?

Heaven lies about us in our infancy,

  And heaven is not a thing of sight or sense ;

Here on this desolate flower-forsaken lea

  It opens to the eyes of innocence :

There is an Eden for us all, till we

  Let in a devil who straightway drives us

  thence.

"THY WILL BE DONE."

A Painting by Sir Noel Paton.

——o——

I.—THE PAINTING.

" No earthly beauty shines in him,
To draw the carnal eye."

'Twas in the painter's choice: he might have
     framed
A figure more commanding, and a face
Earthlier fairer and of finer grace,
And none that loves the Saviour would have
     blamed.
But wiser he: so should a form that aimed
     At drawing all men to him take a place
     No ways superior to the common race,
In proof he was not of their state ashamed.
And so—no hero, cased as if in mail
     With adventitious halo of romance;

No strong-built athlete, never known to ail,
  Proud of his strength, defiant in his glance;
But looking as if liable to fail,
  With nothing to commend him or enhance.

II.—TO THE PAINTER.

Creator of The Christ! when first I stood
  Before thy handiwork, and overawed
  Beheld the mystery of the Son of God
Sinless yet suffering in the midnight wood,
Suffering, and yet to suffering quite subdued,
    How could I think of thee? how could I
      laud
    The power that pained me so? or how
      applaud
In presence of that brow with blood bedewed?

And yet I owe a dearer debt to thee
  Than I have paid to any: there will rise
Within my memory Paul; yet even he,
  The great Apostle, failed to *realise*

As thou hast done, for thou hast made me see
    The Christ in Scotland with my actual eyes!

Great Painter! unto thee the awful dower
    Of genius has been given to dare and do,—
    To image Deity in pain, pursue
The image into act, hour after hour,
And bid it live! I tremble for the power,
    God-lent and (surely for great ends) to few,
    That thus creates the agony anew
Which God hid in Gethsemanë's dark bower!

—For they will come, the idle and the rude,
    And these will praise thy skill, and those
        will blame;
And some, indulgent of a prying mood,
    Will stand and stare, departing as they
        came;
And thou wilt seem, thy work misunderstood,
    In these to put the Lord to open shame!

P

TENANTLESS.

A LEVEL waste, where sheep are starving drear,
And lapwings breed, and sapless windle-
    straws,
Weakly submissive to the gusty flaws,
For ever round the waste forlornly veer,—
In midst whereof, most desolate, appear
    Four grey walls round an empty house : you
        pause
    As you pass by, and ask what fool he was
That built, and brought his household darlings,
    here ?
No pathway through the waste leads to the door
    That fronts the snow-cold hills ; the lake
        between,
    When, as to-day, a north wind's blowing keen,
Sends to the very doorstep, cold and hoar,
    Patches of flying foam :—a dreary scene !
Thank heaven ! to be lived in by child no
    more !

WELL, this is what I saw on Granton pier :
In front, the Firth !—"Oh, that is nothing
new ! "
Ay, but you never saw a bonnier blue
Than its glad waters wore ; the day was clear,
And—you may laugh—to me they seemed to
rear
Their waves in actual joy ! Now, *this* is true—
One of the waves took wings, became a mew,
And sunward rose upon a new career !
Across the Firth I saw the coast of Fife
With here a cliff and there a nestling town :
And here and there the hillsides showed the
strife
Of April green contesting winter brown ;
And eastward far the horizon's edge was rife
With clean white sails that rose and sank
adown.

ON LOMOND HILL.

THE top at last ! . . . All hail, celestial blue !
  Mother of Freedom, where the winds are nurst
  And the clouds fly, and sunbeams through
    them burst,
Gilding this old earth till it shines anew !
From thy broad bosom also drops the dew
  As duly on the grass as at the first
  Ere storms were known, and the green earth
    was curst,
And Man from Nature within walls withdrew.
—Yonder, far o'er the Firth, what smoky blot
  Stains the pure ether?   Ah! I know it: there
The Town-Witch, crooning o'er her seething-
    pot,
  Compounds and brews for man infernal fare!
Thee and thy stews, black Witch ! from this
    high spot
  I solemnly for one whole week forswear !

TWO SONNETS IN DEFENCE OF SONG.

*

I. MORNING.

LOOSE beechen leaves above me; over which,
   The cupola of heaven—so still and bright,
With the sun dreaming in a far high niche,
   You think it never can again be night.
Nature at rest. The only sounds that reach
   The listening ear are Labour's, and are
      light—
Rustlings among the oats, the reaper's speech,
   And the mill-hum of a small town in sight.
Afield and in the factory they work,
   Those at the loom, and these among the
      corn;
While I, the only idler, seem to shirk
   The duty laid on every one that's born,
And, lapt in leaves, among the beeches lurk,
   A spy upon my fellows all the morn.

II. EVENING.

But evening comes : the sounds of Labour
    cease,
And weary workers from their toil return ;
Domestic lights in cottage windows burn,
And sundered families unite in peace.
Now what shall smooth with gentle hand the
    crease
Of furrowed brow and ruffled heart outworn,
Strengthen for the recurring toils of morn,
And wrap the spirit in the robes of peace?
—Song ! which the poet, idling, as ye said,
    Gathered fresh-fallen from the morning skies.
Song ! which he wove, and dipped in rainbow
    dyes
When ye cried *Out upon him, Lazyhead !*
Song ! that both feeds and clothes, and far
    outvies
Your factory fabrics and your oaten bread !

BERRY-HILL.

WE stand upon the Ochils in the air
  Of a September eve ; great fleecy clouds,
  Like sheep new - washen, circle earth in
    crowds,
But all the cupola is blue and bare.
Here, on the right, *our* Lomond towers ; and
    there,
  Far to the west, from a pale smoke that
    shrouds
  Its base, Ben Lomond ; and the heaven is
    bowed
Serenely o'er us, resting on the pair.—
It is a dutiful delight to flee
  At times the sorcery of the sordid town,
To shake the mind from all vexations free,
  To know on hill-tops Heaven without
    frown,
And feel like children looking up to see
  Their parents at a window smiling down !

A HUMOUR OF THE LINKS.

HE drops in dapper dress upon the ground,—
  White cuffs, and sleeve-links glancing in the
    sun,
  —A demd fine morning!—this at half-past
    one,—
And with three caddies enters on a round.
He hits the turf; the ball with oblique bound
  Flees to the onlookers, who duck and run,
  And running fall, and falling yell *What fun!*
While he calls *Fore!*—and wonders when 'tis
    found.
Six balls he loses, breaks three clubs, a cleek,
  And, putting, makes an unexpected drive
Which lames a boy and cuts a golfer's cheek,
  And so ends round the first at half-past five—
Seven holes in ninety strokes!—I would not
    seek
  To wrong a living man: the man's alive!

LOCHLEVEN IN NOVEMBER.

MORNING succeeded morning o'er the Lake
  All through the spring, and never once a
    pair
  Came quite the same, and yet the Lake was
    fair
And kept the lengthening charm without a
    break.
And surely now (thought I) no power will take
  Her beauty from the Naiad; none will dare
  To give the honour to the earth or air,
But all will praise it for her own dear sake.
—Well, one November morning, dazed and
    deaved
  With the dull round of the professional
    wheel,
I left the city, and stole unperceived
  Upon my Naiad ere the morning meal:
She looked up hastily, surprised and grieved,
  Like a proud beauty caught in *deshabille!*

THE LAWN-ADONIS.

LAWN-TENNIS and the Ladies—give him these :
    Misses, with rosebud mouths, and creamy
        cheeks
    Spread thinly with a smile that lasts for
        weeks :
And leave the silken Sybarite to his ease.
No other paradise so well could please,
    No other paradise the spaniel seeks ;
    That smirk of well-fed satisfaction speaks
A life content with what it sucks and sees.
—You sneer,' Major ! The sneer upon your
        lip'll
Only bring pouts, my gallant god of war !
What ! to his ruby mouth deny the nipple,
    And smirch his pearls with porter and cigar,
To whom the smell of small beer's a strong
        tipple
And Polson's paste a food too solid far ?

" Nec vixit male, qui natus moriensque fefellit."
— HORACE, *Epist.* xvii.

A GREAT man dies, or whom the world calls
    great
  —And, I've observed, the world will scarce
    allow
One leaf of laurel to your living brow
Though it grows lavish when you lie in state :
This for your comfort,—well, he's dead ! and,
    straight,
  A kite sits on the shroud ; but whence or how
  The carrion came you cannot guess; and now
It claims with yellow beak and claw its bait.
Faugh ! 'Tis enough to make the dead upstart,
  To be so near a living grave, and smell it !
Happy the man who takes the final dart
  And drops among the grass with none to
    tell it,
Who quietly through life has done his part,
  And, to quote Horace, *moriens fefellit!*

OLD AGE—THE WRESTLER.

SEEMS but as yesterday that I was young,
Inhaled the fever of the war of life,
Made eager preparations for the strife,
And with the joy of a strong gymnast flung
My soul into the contest : swayed and swung
This way and that I reeled ; yet joys were
rife,—
Home, and the smile of friends, the love of
wife,
And Hopes that flew above my head and sung.
But, as I wrestled, woe, alas ! my pride
Of youthful strength received a fall from One
Who came upon me with a hasty stride
And threw me heavily: broken, undone,
I rose and to a corner limped aside,
And lo, far down the west had sunk my sun !

WINTER'S PALE MARTYR.

HERE, in the social city, by the hearth,
  This winter midnight, in an easy-chair,
  While the flames bicker on the bars, and
    flare,
And a wild east wind blowing up the Firth
Shouts down the chimney in its boisterous
    mirth,
  Put on your hat and face me if you dare—
  I think me of a hillside lone and bare
Far up among the Ochil Hills of Perth.
How piteously it waited for the spring
  With a cold snow-drop sickening in its hand!
How patiently it waited for the wing,
  That never came, of summer in the land!
And now it stands in snow-shirt shivering,
  Winter's pale martyr, meekly at command!

"A BARBARY HEN."

See SHAKESPEARE'S *As You Like It.*

WHITHER have fled his gamesomeness and glee,

His rosy gills, his laughter, and his jinks,

The sparkle of his eyes between the winks,

And all the merriment we used to see?

There is not now a duller man than he :

At festive times he sits alone and thinks,

Drains glass on glass, and still the more he
drinks

The less inclined to smile he seems to be.

And now, what power in what fell hour did
snatch

The mirth we may not hope to see again?

—They say it went for money in a match

That gave him with the gold *a Barbary Hen!*

—Proves the old proverb, Tom ! the maddest
bach-

Elors make still the saddest married men !

NORWEGIAN SONNETS

To Norroway, to Norroway,
To Norroway owre the faem!
— Old Ballad.

I.

BALDER BACK!

FACING the North, in the grey sea he stands.
  The solar orb comes northward, sliding slow,
  And—empties on him its solstitial glow !
Blinks up at last with tear-bewildered glands
The puzzled jotun :* from his rough red hands
  Slip the huge balls of hard compacted snow
  That in his wrath enraged he meant to throw,
And where they melt, behold ! a brace of vands. †
Meanwhile the blinding tears run down his
     cheeks,
  Like torrents swollen with sudden summer
     rain ;
In vain deep-knuckling in his eyes he seeks
  To clear his sight—the cataracts burst amain ;
Till, at the last, he gets a peep, and speaks
  —*It's you, Balder ! So you've got back again !*

* Giant.   † Lakes.

Q

UP THE SKAGER RACK.

It was the point of dawn; and in the bow
  I stood alone, facing the grey north-east.
  Far on the left, like a huge brown sea-beast
That had been chased and was o'ertaken now,
Surprised asleep, lay Norway.　From the prow
  A hissing of salt spray that still increased
  Rose plainly audible—for the gale had ceased
And the keel cut the sea-plain like a plough.
And so with only a ripple on the sea,
  And ne'er a storm-cloud o'er us muttering
    black,
We voyaged with an easy course and free
  And—disappointing, now on looking back ;
For the old sagas make the surges flee
  Like riderless horses up the Skager Rack.

III.

WELCOME!

Was it the filial instinct of a child
  Yearning to visit the ancestral home
  That drove me o'er the furrows and the foam
To Norway northward of the ocean wild?
Meseemed at least from fell on fell up-piled
  Streamed voices—*Now at last, though late,*
    ye come;
  Here is your parent land, no longer roam :
And the scenes grew familiar all, and smiled.
But who was he, this worshipper of Thor?
  Or, likelier, Odin would the genius suit
Of a bold-cruising Viking ancestor—
  Some scale-mailed Eric, or chain-shirted
    Knut!
—Vainly I questioned welcoming breeze and
    torr,*
  The winds were silent now, the mountains
    mute!

        * Hill.

IV.

THAT SPEAR.

WE parted with the *Times* at Guldsmedmo'n,
Yet two days longer up the dale the hum
Of European politics would come—
But sunk, and sinking, to an undertone.
At last we entered a deep dell o'ergrown
With ancient pines of lofty stature—some
An hundred feet—and Europe's voice was
    dumb,
And we now fairly found ourselves alone.
Silence, and gloom, and isolation drear
Produced a feeling, hard to understand,
Which grew at last a dim-embodied fear
As of a Spirit, gloomy, silent, grand,
That rose from out the wood, and drew a-near,
Grasping a pine-spear in his rebel hand !

V.

MILTON IN NORWAY.

The feeling passed, the Spirit passed away
  —The silence and the isolation drear,
  As broke in fitful bursts on Fancy's ear
A gravely measured yet melodious lay.
Wider the sweep, and more complete the sway,
  And longer, deeper, louder, and more clear,
  Until I cried—*Milton is monarch here,*
Whatever Oscar and his subjects say!
—How had the Master slung into his song
  The pride of Norway, with an arm as free
As fierce Alcides' when he hurled along
  The ether from Mount Œta to the sea,
Nerved with the strength of that Thessalian
    wrong,
  The groaning trunk of many an uptorn tree !

VI.

THE SCENERY—GO AND SEE IT!

AND speak ye may of grandeur and of gloom
And all the dread magnificence that lies
Where through the dale the foam - fleckt
torrent flies,
Or gorgeous sunsets o'er the mountains bloom.
But who shall in the sonnet's scanty room
Set the majestic magnitude, the size,
The mighty mountains and the widening
skies
Up on Norwegian table-lands assume?
This you must see to feel within your heart,
And cannot know from others: Nature still
In this defies all imitative art,
Baffles all schools and soars beyond their
skill:
It is a joy she only shall impart,
But, once received, it ne'er can cease to thrill.

VII.

A TERROR OF THE TWILIGHT.

FAR in Norwegian solitudes we strayed :
  Behind us lay a long bright summer day,
  But evening now was stooping o'er our way,
When, at a sudden turn, alarmed we stayed.
It was a terror by the twilight made
  Of river, cliff, and cloud, and the weird play
  Of sunset's one live liberated ray
Piercing the horror of the pinewood shade.
Stood, like a charred cross, or a huge sword-
      hilt,
  Against the sky, above the cliff's black line,
That seemed a bastion by Harfager built,
  A solitary thunder-blasted pine ;
On the dark flood below, the sunset spilt
  What now was blood and now was wassail-
      wine.

VIII.

A WATERFALL WITHIN A WOOD.

THE sound, that seemed at sunrise—when the
   glow
Of Morning, mingling with the early breeze,
Caught the still water through the lakeside
   trees—
The Voice of Liberty, now seems to grow
The muffled moan of an imprisoned woe ;
   And Fancy, peering through the forest, sees
   An agonising Samson on his knees,
With the pines looking on and whispering low.
How does a noise, monotonous and rude,
   Take tone, when blown into a poet mind,
Concording with the mystery of its mood,
   And suiting with the symphony it designed !
—'Tis but a waterfall within a wood
   To Peter Bell and others of his kind.

IX.

MINERVA IN THE SÆTERSDAL.

WE said *Far Vel* to Frœsnæs at the dawn—
   Leaving it as one leaves a treasure, soon
To long for it, and call it prize and boon
In words, sincere no doubt, but overdrawn.
Then on we raced as gamesome as the fawn
   Though not so graceful, till mid-afternoon
Brought us to Hellé to the skydsstation *
Under a cliff behind a natural lawn.
Here in a squalid room we look for ease,
   Loath to sit down, but yet too tired to stand,
And call for black-cock, bacon, bread and cheese
   —In short, whate'er their larder might com-
      mand :
Enters Minerva, kilted to the knees,
   With a vast shield of fladbröd in her hand !

---

* Pronounced *shüs-stashöön*—the posting-station.

X.

THE LITTLE MEAL-MILL.

PERCHED on its four grey cairns across the
    stream
That tumbles down the cliff, secure it stands;
An old possession, for on plank and beam
    Are Knuts and Olës carved by various hands.
Its cubic measure, six by five by four;
    Yet in this compass, everything complete;
And there he bent—his back was towards the
    door—
While plashed the mill-wheel merrily at his
    feet,
And ground his rye, and sang with honest glee.
    —Be mine the knowledge that I now possess,
And mine a heart, like his, of envy free,
    And I could don to-day the sæter* dress,
And bring my wishes docile to my will
To moil content in this Norwegian mill.

* A sæter is a farm: the sæter dress, the dress of the peasants
of the Sætersdal.

XI.

THE CLIMB FROM VALLË.

STEEP was the climb from Vallë: far below
   The sæter we had left lay lost in mist,
   And still the height rose higher than we wist
Beyond the ravings of the Otteraa.*
And now a thin bleak air began to blow,
   And now the bispevei† to turn and twist,
   Here round a tjern ‡ no summer ever kissed,
And there behind a hide of hoarded snow.
The stars dissolved anon; and airy trills
  Of wavering music showed the day begun:
We toiled to meet the morn—o'er rocks, o'er
     rills;
  And, breathless, but at last our wish we won—
The top! and lo, a countless herd of hills
  Tossing their shining muzzles in the sun!

     * Pronounced Ottero.   † Bridle-path.
         ‡ Mountain lake, tarn.

XII.

"PAA HEJA:" LIFE ON THE HEIGHTS.

Is there a pleasure can with this compare?—
  To leap at sunrise from your mountain-bed,
  Roused by a skylark revelling overhead,
And drink great draughts of golden morning
    air;
A plunge, and breakfast—simple rural fare;
  Then forth with vigorous brain, elastic tread,
  Hope singing at your heart o'er sorrow dead,
And strength for fifty miles, and still to spare!
That joy was ours!—O memory! oft restore us
  Those autumn runs, here in the smoky town,
When through the woods our mad nomadic
    chorus
  Rang freedom up and civilisation down!
Io! my hearts! the world was all before us,
  And we nor owned nor envied king nor
    crown!

XIII.

THE MOUNTAIN LAUREATE.

MORNING is flashing from a glorious sun
  On the broad shoulders of the giant fells
  That outreach arms across the narrow dells
And form a silent brotherhood of one
Listening their skylark laureate ! New begun
  He up the heavens in ever-rising swells
  Carries their thanksgiving in song that wells
From his small breast as if 'twould ne'er be
    done.
What life his music gives them ! They are
    free
  In the wild freedom of his daring wing ;
And in the cataract of his song, the sea
  Of poetry that fills all heaven, they sing ;
—He is their poet-prophet in his glee,
  And in his work and worth their priest and
    king !

XIV.

A THOUGHT OF HOME.

SHE walks where Callerfountain to Kinnoull
Looks lovingly across the twists of Tay,
And oft, along the zigzag of her way,
Up Craigie burn, or through the plantains
  cool,
Stoops, from the bank beside the shaded pool
To pluck forget-me-nots, or from the brae
A gowan, with whose petals she will play,
Filling her breast of love's distractions full.
Fair are the Scottish hills around her here,
  Nor fairer scenes a wandering eye beheld,
But now in all the glory of the year
  To her their beauty is a dream of eld,
And Norway's distant hills have grown more
  dear
  —For sake of one far up the Dovrefeld.

XV.

MORNING—THE MOUNTAIN FAMILY AT THEIR DEVOTIONS.

I SEE across the lofty table-lands
  A hundred regal mountains at the least
  Inclining mutely towards the opening East,—
As many little tjerns and queenly vands
Kneeling at different levels: Phœbus stands
  Beaming benevolence like a great High Priest
  Blessing a nation for some holy feast
At his wide temple-door with lifted hands.—
Rejoice, ye hills ! ye happy mountains, fling
  Your arms aloft in worship wildly free !
Ye vands, and rivers in the valleys, sing !
  Shout ! till the heavens ring with your choral
    glee ;
And God Himself with mild face wondering
  Looks out at last, and smiles well-pleased to
    see !

XVI.

A CANDIDATE FOR HONOURS.

THIS were a spectacle to cleanse the heart
Of all the mean vexations of the town,
The envious slander and the jealous frown,
And all remembrances that make it smart.
Phœbus Apollo ! fit another dart
And shoot the last surviving meanness down
Ere on my head thou place the golden crown
And teach my lyre the mystery of thine art !
Then, with a bosom purified of hate
And rankling cares and cankers reared of
wrong,
Envy forgotten and the low debate
That to unworthy rivalry belong,
On thine own heights, Apollo, will I wait
A shriven candidate of holy song !

XVII.

"THE LAST INFIRMITY."

THE god !—or else a fierce consuming flame !
 Spare me, Apollo of the burning brow !
 Spare me ! It was a rash novitiate's vow
When to thy shrine with shameful haste I came
And vowed, alas ! with an unworthy aim,
 To be a priest of thine : forgive me now
 And let me go, or take me where I bow
And purge me of that lust of earthly fame !
—Thus, like a weed that woos the summer sun
 To wither in the fierceness of his glance,
The ignoble wish that I had told to none
 And scarcely to myself, by sweet mischance,
Seeking to honour it, was clean undone,
 Pierced by Apollo's keen detecting lance.

R

XVIII.

HARVEST IN THE DALE.

A MILLION fields to-day are standing white
Over the north of Europe: here is one,
And three bright sickles circling in the sun
Will have the little crop cut down ere night.
The girl is singing, for her heart is light;
But the two brothers think it best to shun
The guise of gladness till the work be done
And they have earned a reason and a right;
Yet they are glad: God of the bounteous Year,
What pleasure must be Thine to look from
heaven
Into a thousand happy dales, and hear
From out the barren rocks, where man has
striven,
The voices of Thy children far and near
Rejoicing in the gifts which Thou hast given!

XIX.

ARTHUR'S SEAT AGAIN!

FJORD, wood, and waterfall, and cliff whose line
   Rose level with the heavens, and the long
      swell
Of fell up-reaching arm to brother fell,
And the lone aspiration of the pine
That stood erect on sunset heights divine
   Under the gaze of God in holy spell,
   While on the slope, or from the sunken dell,
Aspens looked up and trembled—these were
      mine ;
And I had grown familiar with them till
   They seemed a patrimony all my own ;
And yet when Arthur's green and rounded hill
   Met my returning gaze, and seaward blown
A Scottish voice came floating—closer still
   Was Scotland at my heart than I had known.

XX.

A GREY MORNING AT GRANTON.

" How bright it is to-day! we see across
  The Firth quite clearly to the shores of Fife ! "
  —Good heavens !   And yet *'twere pity of my
    life*

(Thought I, while travelling northward to
    Kinross)

If I should count as worse to me than loss
  My fellow - creature's gain.   Yet was the
    strife

'Twixt scorn and pity for the grey-worn wife,
Thankful for nothing as it seemed, a toss.
For I had been where skies of brilliant hue
  Soared o'er gigantic cliffs to heaven itself,
Where the delighted eye for miles looked thro'
  Opaline widths of air, and aa * and elv †
Linked vand to fjord with chains of living blue,
  Or shot in foam from granite shelf to shelf !

Water; pronounced *o*.   † Stream; pronounced *elf*.

XXI.

ON THE PIER AT BURNTISLAND.

So ran my thoughts at Granton as the train
    Swept curving round in view of the grey sea,
    But when the lazy steamer crossed, and we
Were free of its collective stinks again,
I caught a glimpse, through cloud, coal-smoke,
        and rain
    Upon the sloppy pier, that furnished me
    The missing gloss there well was need to be
To clear the air for her, and light the main !—
The world looks bright to kings—a favoured
        race
    Who free of toil through earth's gay gardens
        roam ;
Looks fair to lovers; and a happy place
    To children ; but its brightest mornings come
To humble mother waiting the embrace
    Of her bronzed sailor son returning home.

XXII.

A RARE DIP.

I'VE floated on Lochleven, dipped in Tay,
  And many another stream both great and
    small,
  Dared the white thunder of a waterfall,
And been baptised in many a mill-wheel's
    spray;
I've drunk the brine in Kristiania bay
  And swum almost all up the Sætersdal.
  And every bath was ecstasy, but all
Must yield to one rare dip I had to-day.
Oh, pleasantly the Farg's clear waters flashed
  Into the rocky pool their liquid song;
With more than Alpheus' haste I stripped, and
    dashed
  Among the music, plunging oft and long;
And not alone my limbs—the music washed
  Hate from my heart, and from my memory
    wrong!

XXIII.

FROM THE WICKS OF BAIGLIE.

HERE there are braes, and glens, and brawling
   brooks,
   And cascades flinging loose their diamond
      spray,
   And waters winding down to firth and bay,
And woods, and craigs, and knowes, and fairy
      nooks;
But on the hill-tops there are golden stooks,
   And mill-wheels in the cascade's thunder play,
   Boats breast the river, artists glenward stray,
And over barren craigs rise pastoral crooks.—
Not many years ago the scene was claimed
   By the rude elements—to whom it gave
Thistle, and thorn, and stone, and stream un-
      named,
   Harvestless hill, and undivided wave;
Now the wild elephant is trapped and tamed,
   Caparisoned and tended—and a slave!

XXIV.

THELEMARKEN : A PER-CONTRA.

However, there's the freedom of the Fells,
Such as the wilds of Thelemarken show,
Where cataracts roar unbridged, and torrents
flow
Burdened but with the beauty of their bells ;
Where the cliff soars, and the broad sky-roof
swells,
And morning comes with larger longer glow,
And, pinnacled beyond the axe's blow,
In peace the stately pine its centuries tells !
Here you may live at large, with no one nigh :
—Only, when twilight darkens earth and air,
From the lone uplands you may chance to spy
On the cliff-edge a wolf, perhaps a pair ;
Or silhouetted on the evening sky
The slouching horror of a hermit bear !